Called Harry

First published in 2010 by Scholastic New Zealand Limited
Private Bag 94407, Botany, Manukau 2163, New Zealand

Scholastic Australia Pty Limited
PO Box 579, Gosford, NSW 2250, Australia

ISBN 978-1-86943-970-5

National Library of New Zealand Cataloguing-in-Publication Data

---

Werry, Philippa, 1958-
A girl called Harry / by Philippa Werry.
ISBN 978-1-86943-970-5
[1. Imagination—Fiction. 2. Creative ability—Fiction. 3. Schools
—Fiction.] I. Title.
NZ823.2—dc 22

12 11 10 9 8 7 6 5 4 3 2 1 0 1 2 3 4 5 6 7 / 1

Publishing team: Diana Murray, Penny Scown and Annette Bisman
Cover design: Vida Kelly
Typeset in Stone Informal 10.5/16pt by Book Design Ltd www.bookdesign.co.nz

Printed and bound in Australia by McPherson's Printing Group

Scholastic New Zealand's policy, in association with McPherson's Printing Group, is to use papers that are renewable and made efficiently from wood grown in sustainable forests, so as to minimise its environmental footprint.

A Girl Called Harry

PHILIPPA WERRY

SCHOLASTIC
AUCKLAND SYDNEY NEW YORK LONDON TORONTO
MEXICO CITY NEW DELHI HONG KONG

This book is for Brooklyn School
teachers, staff and students,
and families, past and present.

All characters are of course entirely fictitious!

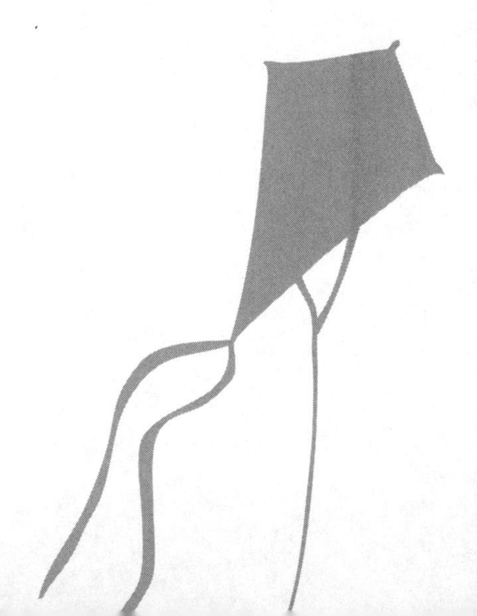

Chapter One

"LOOK! NEW GIRL!" JESSICA SQUEALED.

The day the new girl arrived, we were the first ones to see her. We were Official New Girl Spotters. We got to hang around the door of our classroom, waiting for everyone else to arrive – Piper, Aleesha, Tina, Zoe, Renee, Latisha (not Claudine, of course) – and when they turned up, we passed on the news before they could see for themselves. "Guess what? New girl!"

They were as excited as we were. Not the boys, of course, they weren't excited at all.

"Not another girl," Karl Ballentyne groaned. "There's too many already. Can we send her back?"

We saw her first because Jessica was ready on time for once, so we got to school early, and spotted her through the classroom windows. There she was, with her parents, talking to Mr Cool and the principal, Mr Bennett. Her dad was in there, anyway. I couldn't see her mum, but she might have been trying to keep out of the principal's way as he flapped his arms around, explaining what a fantastic school it was.

Yeah, right, her mum would be thinking, *a fantastic school, run by a lunatic who thinks he's a giant flamingo.*

The new girl looked a lot like her dad. They were both tall, although she wasn't quite as tall as Jessica, and they both had thin, sharp faces. But I didn't pay him much attention after that first glance, because I was too busy watching her – the new girl – looking round at the stuff on the walls. Our Family Tree posters were still on display, and I wondered if she was looking at mine, because it certainly stood out, whatever Mr Cool and Karl Ballentyne said about it. My Family Tree poster stood out a lot more than I did. The new girl might not notice me, but there was a chance that she might notice the poster. "That looks interesting," she might think. "I wonder who drew that."

"New girl! I love new girls!" Jessica squealed again.

This was back in the time when Jessica and I still did things together, before she stopped talking to me and started treating me like I didn't exist, or, if I did, it was only as some juvenile and unimportant life form, like a caterpillar or a tadpole.

"What's her name?" Jessica said. "Who's she sitting next to?"

"Let's go and ask if we can look after her." *I* actually *said* that. It was *my idea.* I didn't even get suspicious when Jessica charged into the classroom and called out, "She can sit next to me. Harry won't mind moving."

What? I thought. Jessica and I always sat together. But we were both in welcoming-new-girls mode, and I hadn't had second thoughts yet. I was still on my first thoughts, which were *New girl, yay!*

How do you tell when your second thoughts start overtaking your first thoughts? Is there a split second when you see them passing? Or do you only realise later?

That's what happened to me. I didn't notice the exact moment when my second thoughts zoomed ahead. But a week or two later, they were so far in front that they could have got a speeding ticket.

Chapter Two

"GOOD MORNING, ROOM NINE," MR Cool said. "This is Mallory," and a murmur swept round the class as all the girls went *Ooh, Mallory, I like her name. I don't know any other Mallorys,* they whispered to each other; *yeah, it's really unusual but I like it, don't you?*

This was a little annoying, because in our class I'm the one with the unusual names. There's not much else that's unusual about me, but my names are: not Harry, but all my other names.

Harry is only unusual because some people think it isn't a girl's name. In fact, the very first thing I can remember about Karl Ballentyne (apart from when he hit me after I sprained my wrist) is him staring at me in kindergarten saying, "That's a *boy's* name. Why have you got a *boy's* name? That girl's got a *boy's* name," he kept telling any other kid who came near. "That girl's got a *boy's* name," he told his dad when he came to pick him up, and his dad, who is a lot more sensible than Karl, said, "No, I expect it's just short for something." But the next day Karl came straight over to me and said, "Have you *still* got a boy's name?"

I'm not totally sure if I remember that or not, but it's one of those stories that's gone down in family history. Mum used to work as a chef in Karl's dad's restaurant, and between meals they would sit round talking about their kids, and all the funny things they'd ever done, which are more like silly and embarrassing things if you're the one doing them, and things that you wish other people would forget. So that story might get retold in the Ballentyne household too, although I sincerely hope not.

Harry isn't a boy's name, because it's short for Harriet. One year I tried spelling it Harri on all my school books, or even Harrie, but that just looked dumb, like I'd forgotten how to spell the ending of my own name.

Anyway, Jessica wasn't annoyed. She beamed, as though she was entitled to some of the limelight, because the new girl with the unusual name was sitting next to her.

"Mallory . . ." and then Mr Cool made a noise like a machine breaking down: "Woz-ziz-click-jetski," it sounded like, and all the girls went *Ooh, Woz-ziz-splutter-something, what an amazing surname!*

This was even more annoying, because "Woz-ziz-click-jetski" might be impossible to spell, or to pronounce, but it was definitely more unusual than McDonald. So the big question was, how many names did she have *altogether*? Was I still ahead in total name count? I would have to find out.

We call him Mr Cool, but that's not his real name. He's Angus Cameron. But he is definitely the coolest teacher at school, despite the potential geek-factor of a name like Angus. He's tall, good-looking, zooms around in a red sports car, and once promised to have his head shaved if the school raised over $500 in a coin trail for Charity Week.

Jessica and I were in charge of Charity Week because we were in the Charities team. This was one of the principal's Bright Ideas – Leadership

Teams, to make us into the Leaders of the Future. Like most of his other Bright Ideas, it didn't work. All it did was make everyone squabble about which teams they did or didn't want to be in. But Jessica and I were lucky, because we got Charities, which was fun and the one everyone wanted.

We went around every class, reminding them to bring their gold coins, and we raised $645 ... or possibly more, because I think I lost a bag of two-dollar coins somewhere, although I never told Jessica that. Anyway, it was enough, and the two of us got to help shave his hair off in the playground, with everyone else standing round screaming. Zoe Watson screamed so loudly she started to hyperventilate, and had to go to the medical room and lie down for the rest of the day.

Some men with bald heads look like complete losers, but Mr Cool looked even cooler than before. He hasn't grown his hair back, either. If it's hot and sunny he wears a baseball cap, or a beanie if it's cold.

"Now then, let me guess," he continued, once everyone had settled down from craning to look at Mallory-with-the-unusual-name-and-amazing-surname. "How many of you—"

"Morning, Mr Cameron," Zoe Watson called out. "I like your red shirt . . ."

"Thanks, Zoe," Mr Cool said, "so do I. How many of you—"

"Only I'm not quite sure if the tie goes with it," Zoe went on.

"Of course it does," said Jessica, our in-house fashion expert. "Black goes with everything," she said, in her usual *who-doesn't-know-that* manner.

"But there are flecks of orange in it," Zoe pointed out, "and orange doesn't always go with red. Did Carmen think it matched?"

Zoe is not really interested in colour matching, but she is a total Mr Cool fan. She's President of MCAS (the Mr Cool Appreciation Society) and spends more time investigating his love life than doing her schoolwork. MCAS members call it Appreciation, but it's more like Adoration, and it's the reason that lots of our lessons get sidetracked. Because Carmen was a new girlfriend, Zoe was trying to find out as much as she could about her. She thought she was being subtle, when she was about as subtle as an orange tie.

Personally, I thought I already had a pretty good idea of what Carmen would be like. Spanish, obviously, with a name like that . . . very beautiful . . . and probably an opera singer as well . . . but also a top soccer player, which is what attracted Mr Cool to her in the first place. She would want to go back to Spain eventually, though. They would get married and have a whole team of soccer-playing children, and Mr Cool would have to learn to speak Spanish, which could be a problem, judging from the difficulty he had in trying to teach us to say hello in Chinese.

"Carmen gave it to me," Mr Cool said. (I could have predicted that. Carmen was stylish as well.) "Now, as I was saying – or trying to – how many of you did some work on your new topic over the weekend?"

Our new topic was Conservation, and we were supposed to pair up, research an endangered animal and present our findings to the class. Zoe wasn't listening, because she was too busy contemplating Mr Cool's orange-and-black tie, and thinking about Spanish Carmen. Jessica wasn't listening, because she had left the choice of our animal up to me. Plus, she was busy giving Mallory a potted history of everyone in our class, including confidential information on their popularity and fashion ratings. I wasn't going to score very highly on either of those. Nobody else answered, because nobody had done any work on anything.

"Yeah, well, I couldn't," Karl said at last. "I was playing soccer all weekend."

"*All* weekend?" Any other teacher would have told Karl off for obvious exaggeration, but Mr Cool looked seriously impressed. "What was this, some sort of nonstop, 48-hour soccer-a-thon?"

This is typical of our class environment, which is heavily biased towards sport. Mr Cool actually supported the idea of someone wasting their entire weekend playing soccer.

"Well, yeah, sort of," Karl smirked. "See, we had to prepare for the match, and organise transport to the field, and have a pre-match team talk, and play the game. Then we had the after-match evaluation, and the after-match team function."

In other words, they had to pile into some poor parents' cars, boast about how many goals they were going to score, run round and get incredibly muddy, boast about how many goals they *had* scored, and guzzle lots of soft drink afterwards.

"Did you win?" someone called.

"Well, yeah," Karl said. "Obviously." Unfortunately, his team is quite good and they usually do win, which is even more annoying.

Mr Cool raised one eyebrow, which is a particularly cool trick that he has. The boys always try to copy it, but they can never do it quite right, and it drives the members of MCAS wild. Zoe Watson tried to smother a squeak of excitement.

"I see. So we can take it you're not really interested in the environment, Karl?"

"Sure I am," Karl said. "I'm extremely interested in the environment of the soccer field." Everyone groaned.

Tina put her hand up and said shyly, "I am going to do the tiger. They have tigers where I come from."

"Good idea, Tina," Mr Cool said. "Who's the other one in your pair?"

"Nobody," said Tina, once she'd worked out what he meant. "Just me."

"Let's see, then. Jessica, have you chosen your endangered animal yet?"

"What?" said Jessica, who was giving Mallory the run down on Charities, why it was the best team, the gold coin fundraiser, how we got to shave Mr Cool's hair off and what colour his sports car was. "No," she said, once Mr Cool had repeated the question, "because Harry's going to—"

"All right, why don't you pair up with Tina? And Mallory, you can pair up with Harry."

"*I'll* pair up with Mallory," Jessica said quickly.

"Already sorted," Mr Cool said smoothly. Jessica frowned. She edged her chair a few centimetres closer to Mallory, as if to take over a bit more territory.

And that's exactly how it started to happen, without me even noticing. Centimetre by centimetre.

Chapter Three

JESSICA AND I HAD PAIRED UP FOR YEARS, and I always ended up doing most of the work, so I wasn't too bothered, back then. I didn't mind if she went with Tina for once.

What I was thinking was that tigers, elephants, pandas – all the usual choices – had been taken, but why go for something obvious? Wasn't there an endangered giant snail? Some people had been in the news, protesting over some coal mine that was going to threaten its habitat and maybe cause its extinction. The question was whether a snail was more important than a coal mine, which of course it was, but the mine owners didn't see it that way.

I could cut out a snail-shaped piece of card, and make the writing go in circles inside the shell. That might be a bit hard to read, but it would *look* good.

What about the Loch Ness monster? Did that count as an endangered animal? Or even better, you could *make one up.* Some kind of exotic parrot or deep-sea fish, so endangered that it didn't even exist, except in people's imagination.

Mr Cool wrote **Tina and Jessica – Tiger** up on the board. "Any other creative excuses?" he said. His eyes roved round the classroom, then came to a stop, and one eyebrow went up again.

It was me he was looking at, and I knew exactly why.

Mr Cool and I have a running battle over my projects. I spend hours over them, and they are always the most beautiful looking projects in the whole class. They have original formats and beautiful borders and stunning (if I say so myself, because everyone else does) illustrations. The principal holds them up at assembly, and often they end up on display in the library or in the office, where all the parents admire them as well.

But Mr Cool doesn't see them that way. For some reason, he doesn't share the general enthusiasm where my projects are involved.

Take my Family Tree, for example. A perfect example of my and Mr Cool's differing attitudes to project creation. You could easily spot it among all the other ordinary looking projects up on the walls, and I hoped New-Girl Mallory had. We had to draw our Family Trees at the beginning of the year for Mr Cool. The teachers always ask us to do something like that so they can find out about us, and it gets a bit boring, year after year. You'd think they could just swap notes. Even better, our very first 'All About Me' project could follow us through the school, right from New Entrants to Year Eight. We could simply add an annual update of any significant events, which would speed up the whole process and be far more efficient.

Anyway, most of the teachers already know something about us. It doesn't work for me, being an only child, but take Karl, for example. He's a Ballentyne, so if you know anything about his two older brothers, you have a fair idea of what he's going to be like. Only worse.

But Mr Cool needed the Family Trees because he was fairly new himself, so he didn't know much about us, or our older brothers and sisters. Last year we used to see him taking soccer games at lunchtime, and I thought that was because he'd got landed with all the boring stuff that no other teachers wanted to do, being the newest member of staff. That was before I realised that he *liked* taking soccer games. He would even *race kids back to class* when the bell went, which is a total waste of energy.

Some kids dashed off their Family Trees in ten minutes. Some of them used ready-made templates downloaded from genealogy sites on the Internet. But why call it a tree, if it doesn't look like one? I decided to make mine look like a Christmas tree. I would do each side of the family in Christmas colours, red for the Mabeys on Mum's side, and green for the McDonalds on Dad's side. I would write everyone's names inside little decorations hanging from the branches, and I made miniature presents to go around the base of the tree, real little boxes that I folded up and stuck on, and lots of tinsel and glitter.

It looked great, but the only problem was that I ran out of time, and when it came to finishing it off at school, I couldn't quite remember how all the family fitted together.

Family Trees start off quite easy but quickly become complicated the further back you go, or sideways. Uncle Theo was clear enough, but on Dad's side he has heaps of brothers and half-brothers and stepsisters and cousins living up north, who we hardly ever see. So I have to admit, the names weren't connected in any logical sort of way, but who cares about logic? It *looked* great.

Mr Cool stood and looked at it for a long time. "Harry," he said at last, "this is—" *Beautiful? Creative? Astonishing and fantastic?* "—this is beautiful and creative, but it doesn't tell me much about how everyone in your family is related."

The boys were all standing up on chairs to see, and sniggering.

"Always knew there was something funny about you," Karl said. "So that's it. Turns out you're your dad's aunty."

"Ha ha. Very funny," I said.

Callum pointed at the decoration with Uncle Theo's name on it. "Your uncle's not red, he's a professor. He should be wearing one of those stupid black gowns."

"Yeah, and one of those stupid flat hats with the tassels," Karl said.

I wished I'd thought of that. A black tassel to mark Uncle Theo's name was a brilliant idea. I could have got one from the two-dollar shop, but it was annoying that Karl had thought of it first.

"Is her uncle a professor?" asked Matt, who was still fairly new, and didn't know these things.

"He's a world-famous professor," Karl said, "and her mum's a world-famous chef. That's why Harry's so incredibly clever, and such a brilliant cook, coz it runs in the family. Remember those biscuits she made at Food Tech last year?"

"You mean the concrete ones?" Callum said.

"Ha ha, very funny," I said again, but they were laughing their heads off and didn't hear me.

Later that day the principal came in for some reason, probably unimportant, and while he was having a look round, he made a beeline for my Christmas tree. He was wearing a yellow tie and black jumper, which made his beeline look even more authentic.

"Hmmm. Yes ... very creative!" he said, and Mr Cool made a noise at the back of his throat that sounded suspiciously like *Grrrr!*

Hard luck, Mr Cool, I thought. *Welcome to the wonderful world of my wild imagination. And the sooner you get used to it, the better.*

Chapter Four

"LOOK, HERE COMES CLAUDINE," SOMEONE said, pointing across the playground, as I dragged my attention back from my Family Tree.

"What's happening? What have I missed?" Claudine wanted to know, slinging her swimming bag under her seat. "Who's that?" she asked, staring at Mallory, and Piper leaned over to fill her in.

Mr Cool was still going on about Conservation, so she hadn't missed a lot.

"Remember, for those of you who haven't even started yet," he said, "presentation is important but it isn't everything. Content matters, too."

Content, ha! Who cares about content? You can get

content off the Internet at the last minute, but my illustrations are unique.

"And don't think you can just get your information off the Internet at the last minute," he added, looking round at everyone, but meaning me.

"I didn't get to do any written work over the weekend," I said, to nobody in particular, "but I did quite a lot of practical."

"Yeah, practically going crazy over all your uncle's stupid cats," Karl said. "I guess they're in danger of being patted to death."

"Patting cats is no more crazy than kicking footballs around."

"It's a lot more crazy," Karl retorted. "It's not an Olympic sport, is it? You can't go to the World Cup for kicking cats – I mean, patting them. Oops, sorry – totally unintentional slip of the tongue." Karl Ballentyne drives me up the wall, but I'm used to that. He's been doing it ever since kindergarten.

"So ... what was your after-match team function?" Not that I really cared, but there was no one else to talk to. All the others on our table group had turned their faces towards Mallory, like flowers turned towards the sun. They were totally fascinated by her, as though she was some kind of magnet. Or some kind of snake.

"The usual," he drawled. "Pizza. Laserforce."

This is also typical Karl. Apart from sport, he's only interested in eating and shooting things, either in person or on a computer screen. All the boys went paintballing for his last birthday. And his uncle takes him pig hunting – how totally gross and disgusting is that? Just imagine the blood and the smell. *Yuck.*

I tried hard *not* to imagine the blood and the smell, but I couldn't help it; my imagination was running away with me again. Mum often warns me about that: "Don't let your imagination run away with you, Harry."

Which makes you wonder, what is your imagination like?

Is it something big and fast? Like a lion or an elephant, or maybe a cheetah – cheetahs are very fast – in which case it's not your fault if it runs away with you, because you couldn't stop it. Poor Indian villagers can't help it when they get dragged away and eaten by tigers, can they?

Or is it something little? Like a tiny dog carried round by some celebrity in her handbag, because you *let* it run away with you, but it couldn't run away with you on its own.

Then again, who wants an imagination like a scrawny little dog? And people don't always approve of a wild imagination, but you never hear anyone boasting about having a tame one, do you?

Perhaps imagination is more like a kite, except that nobody ever says, "Don't let your imagination *fly* away with you." On the other hand, they do say "You're getting carried away again," which makes it sound as if the wind is carrying you away, like a balloon or a parachute. They talk about something sparking your imagination, like a match starting a fire. Or they say, a bit disapprovingly, "she can't contain her imagination," as though it's escaping like bread dough spilling out of the top of the breadmaker.

One of my teachers once told Mum, "Harriet lives a bit too much in her imagination," which makes it sound as if it's a country, like France or Spain. (I never liked that teacher much, anyway.) Mr Cool says I have a *vivid* imagination, which sounds colourful. Red, yellow and purple, I think. Perhaps a bit of green. Certainly not brown, black or grey.

I must have been exercising my imagination right then, because Karl said, "No need to pull all those faces. You're just jealous because you're so un-co. There's no way you'll ever make any sort of sports team."

"Oh, excuse me," I said. "I am totally co. You can't be an artist and be un-co. Being an artist is all about coordination; coordinating your brain with your pen or pencil or paints." I looked down at the page of refill in front of me, where there was a picture of a kite with a long, wrinkly string flying through the clouds, although I couldn't remember drawing it. "Of course, that would be difficult for you, because you haven't got much of a brain to coordinate with."

"Listen, Harry, you can't fool me," Karl said, poking me in the side with a blunt pencil. I hate blunt pencils. They're like bitten fingernails. Disgusting. "I can remember you falling off the bars in kindergarten and breaking your arm. They closed the whole playground for a week and we all had to stay inside and do boring stuff with paint and play dough, and I kept getting told off, and it was *all your fault*."

"You got told off because you hit me," I said. "And I did not break my arm. I sprained my wrist. It was a very slight sprain, and there obviously wasn't adequate supervision."

"Nobody else fell off and broke an arm," Karl said. "There was nothing wrong with the supervision." This is one of the problems of going to school with someone who has known you since kindergarten. They know a bit too much about you sometimes.

"So? There's nothing wrong with paint and play dough. If you'd stayed inside and played with them more, you might have a more balanced personality now."

"Harry, Karl ..." Mr Cool said, "could you postpone your debate on the relative merits of the sporting and artistic lifestyles until morning break?"

"Huh? What?" Karl muttered, confused. "We were talking about play dough."

"Who else has chosen their animal?" Mr Cool continued.

"We're going to choose at lunchtime," Jessica said. "We were busy in the weekend."

Busy, yeah right. Shopping.

Chapter Five

WHEN JESSICA SQUEALED, "LOOK! NEW girl!" she was just saying what we all thought. We loved having new girls.

It's not such a big deal for the boys. Matt mooched around on his own for the first few days, getting lost all the time. He didn't even know where the toilets were, because Callum and Karl, who were meant to be looking after him, totally ignored him. The next week, he was down on the bottom field running and yelling his head off with the other boys as if they'd been mates for years, even though he still didn't know their names.

But it's different for girls, and we take it

seriously. We stand round the playground in clumps, until the groups have reorganised and the new girl has slotted into one of them. It's like throwing a pebble into a rock pool and waiting till everything settles down again.

Except that Mallory wasn't like a pebble. She was more like a rock, or a boulder. Or maybe even an avalanche.

The two of us took her round the school, showing her where everything was, pointing out all the teachers and matching them up to their classrooms. Mallory cottoned on pretty quickly, but Jessica wouldn't let up until she'd covered every square metre of the grounds. It was like she wanted everyone to see her *with* Mallory.

For the rest of that week, Jessica stuck to Mallory's side as if fixed there by Superglue. I wondered if it hurt when she peeled herself off at the end of the day. There was a mean little part of me that hoped it did.

We had the school netball trials, and Mallory got into the top team. We had the Athletic Sports, and Mallory won nearly everything. "Mallory runs cross country and plays tennis and water polo, but she's best at netball," Jessica informed us, as if we cared. "Last year, she only just missed out on the rep team, and her netball team did really well. They played in the top grade, and they used to practise three times a week, twice after school and once at lunchtime."

"What position do you play?" Claudine asked.

"Centre," Mallory said.

I wasn't surprised. Somehow I got this feeling that she liked to be right in the middle of whatever was going on. The Centre of Attention, as well as the centre of a netball team.

When she started the whole indoor netball thing, I knew I was right.

"Why doesn't anyone play indoor netball here?" she said, one lunchtime. "Everyone used to play at my old school."

"Why not just play outdoors, like we always do?" Claudine's voice asked from the bottom of a cartwheel.

Mallory explained that you played indoor all year round, and boys could play too. That sounded to me like a drawback, not an advantage, but they all perked up their ears. Well, they didn't *really* perk up their ears. That's what dogs do, although some people can wiggle their ears. What I mean is, they suddenly looked more alert.

"Boys *can* play outdoor netball – if they want to," Aleesha pointed out.

"No, they can't," said Piper.

"Yes, they can, it's in the rules. You can have one or two in a team, but none of them ever wants to. They think they'd look silly," Claudine said.

"They would look silly," I said.

"Lots of boys play indoor netball," Mallory said. "It's a different game, much faster. We need at least six people, and maybe some reserves. I thought we could ask—" and they went into a huddle, listing and comparing names.

Mallory hadn't been at our school very long, but she'd already worked out the team. She'd already worked out that I *wouldn't* be in it, which was fine, because everyone knows that I don't do sport, but I could have decided that for myself. She was captain, naturally, and the rest of the team would be Aleesha, Jessica, Claudine, Piper, Karl, Callum and Matt.

The girls were all keen, although Claudine said she might have to miss some games if she had swim meets. Aleesha said it would only work if the games didn't clash with hockey practice, and Piper added, "Water polo, canoe polo and underwater hockey." Then Piper said, "Who's going to ask the boys?"

"I will," Mallory said.

"Bet they say no," Aleesha said gloomily.

"They won't," Mallory said.

Karl is one of the tallest boys in our class, although that's not saying much, because lots of them are still shrimp-sized, but he and Callum already play basketball. Matt is quite little, but he's fast and good at dodging around other players.

We watched Mallory march up to them and start talking. The boys looked a bit surprised, but she just stood there with her arms folded and waited.

"Bet they won't do it," said Piper.

"They might," said Jessica.

"They might if *Mallory* asks them," said Aleesha.

Matt shrugged and looked at Karl. Callum started playing pretend drums, which is what he always does when he's worried.

"Well ... okay ... I guess ..." Karl wandered over to where we were sitting. Matt followed more slowly, and Callum came behind, still drumming nervously. "So long as we can be called something like the Gladiators," Karl added. "No *girly* team names."

"You could ask Harry," Tina said, as Mallory rejoined our group. "I think she would be good in a team." Tina is the nicest of all the girls. Her

English isn't that good, but it's getting better.

"That shows how little you think," Karl said. "Harriet Weed Washington wouldn't know what a netball was if it hit her on the head."

Matt and Tina both looked puzzled. "Harriet who?" said Tina.

"Which is just why I don't want to play," I said. "That's exactly what you would do, throw the ball right at me."

"Of course we'd throw it at you – and then you're supposed to catch it!" Matt said.

"Give up, Matt," Karl said. "She doesn't understand the finer points of sport."

"Finer points?" Matt said. "All I said was throw and catch." Matt doesn't understand the finer points of sarcasm.

"She doesn't understand *anything* about sport," Karl explained.

"I understand it's a total waste of time," I said, but Karl went on talking as though I wasn't even there.

"She doesn't know what words like 'throw' and 'catch' mean. Anyway, if the ball hit her on the head, it would get lost in her hair." He thrashed around, pretending something was stuck in his own gelled-up hair. "Help! Help! Where is it? Get it out of here!"

Tina was as nice as ever. "You and me can go watch, Harry," she said. "We can cheer. You can be their mascot."

"Yeah, instead of a teddy bear or something. Good one!" Karl yelled back over his shoulder, as they ran off to get their daily fix of mud and adrenaline on the bottom field.

"That's not her real name, is it?" I heard Matt say. "Harriet Weed Washington?"

"Yeah," Karl answered. "Ancient family name. Handed down, you know, like traditional."

"Weird," Matt said, shaking his head.

"So, what *are* we going to be called? I don't want to be a Gladiator," Jessica said, although I don't know why she was complaining. She's had lots of practice in battle, from fighting through the crowds on the first day of the sales.

"You won't have to be. I already registered the name when I signed us up," Mallory said. "We're the Hawaiian Hula Hulas."

"We're *what*?" They all cracked up. "Can't wait to see their faces when they find that out."

"We're *what*?" Karl howled a few days later. "Is this some kind of bad joke?'

"Oh, man! What have you got us into?" Matt said.

"No way!" Callum groaned.

"Too late, sorry," Mallory said. "It's all official now. Anyway," she added with a perfectly straight face, "we thought you'd like it. And it's not as though you have to wear a skirt or anything."

Callum, who hadn't even thought of that possibility, looked even more horrified.

Outdoor netball was boring enough, but at least it was limited to the winter. Once Mallory started up her all-year-round indoor netball team, they could spend endless lunchtimes talking about it. Which team they had played last, who they were playing next, whose parents were taking and bringing them back, who was playing which position.

The prospect of a whole year of netball-related lunchtime conversations unfolded in front of me, like one of those long, straight roads stretching out ahead when you're driving somewhere far away. You don't get carsick on those roads. You just get totally, totally bored.

Chapter Six

"GREAT IDEA!" SAID MR COOL, WHEN HE heard about the indoor netball team, but he'd say that if you organised a team to play anything. Synchronised spaghetti eating, or backward high jump, or underwater five-a-side Pictionary, so long as it could be classed as a sport.

That's the one thing wrong with Mr Cool. As well as being ultra-cool, he is also ultra-sporty.

This makes him almost perfect as far as the sports-mad kids are concerned. Which is most of the boys, especially utterly-sports-crazy Karl Ballentyne, and a few swimmers and tennis players, and all the netball girls.

In other words, it's just about everyone except me. I'm not sporty at all, but this year I've been trapped in a class of sporting fanatics. And, personally, I think the principal made a mistake – one of many – in giving them Mr Cool as a teacher. Much as I like Mr Cool (which is a lot, but not as much as the members of MCAS), I think Mr Bennett should have tried to mould Room Nine into more well-rounded individuals by choosing a teacher who would have emphasised the finer things in life, such as art, and broadened their horizons beyond a netball hoop or a soccer goal. As far as I'm concerned, sport is a waste of time and energy that could be spent in more constructive ways, like drawing, reading or eating chocolate.

Hardly anybody agrees with me, of course. The only other person who is totally uninterested in sport, Zoe Watson, is so besotted by Mr Cool that she'd have a go at anything if he were in charge. She tried out for his water polo team even though she can't swim, and Mr Cool nearly had to dive in and rescue her – but, to her everlasting disappointment, one of the pool's lifeguards got there first.

In my group of friends, or sort-of friends, I am definitely in the minority. Jessica is not over-the-top sporty (this used to be a bond between us) but only because nowadays she'd rather spend all her spare time going shopping. If there was a Leadership Team for Shopping, she'd be in charge of it. She does plays netball because she's so tall, and lately she seems to have been getting even taller, as if she's invented some stretching technique that she's not telling me about. That's hardly fair, considering that I need the extra height more than she does. But Jessica doesn't really share secrets with me any more.

Aleesha plays tennis and hockey – in fact, Aleesha's family *is* hockey at our school. Her dad coaches, her mother manages, and they transport the whole team around in their van. They're really good. Every year they get to the finals, and they nearly always win.

Piper plays water polo, underwater hockey and canoe polo. She's quite little, but fearless. As soon as anything else is invented that involves bashing into other people in the water, she'll play that, too.

Claudine is a top swimmer. She breaks age-group records, has masses of trophies and is always in competitions or going away for swim meets. When she's older she's aiming to swim in the Olympics, and she probably will. Swimming takes up so much of her time that she had to give up gym, but she can still cartwheel all the way across the playground. We all envy Claudine, because she has special dispensation to be late every morning.

"Look, here comes Claudine," someone will say, interrupting Mr Cool droning on, and we look outside and watch her toss her schoolbag aside and go spinning round like a spiralling feather, so lightly her hands hardly seem to touch the ground. She always looks gleaming and freshly washed, and her hair smells of swimming pool chemicals and shampoo.

I'm no good at gym, but I wish I could do cartwheels like that. It would be so cool to be able to see the world upside down, whenever you wanted. And I can see that there might be other advantages in being a good swimmer, apart from the fact that you're allowed to turn up late to school after your training sessions (although having to get up so early might cancel that advantage out).

For example, suppose you were washed overboard in the middle of a shark-infested ocean, it would be useful to be able to swim, whereas it wouldn't be at all useful to be able to shoot a basketball goal. Unless, of course, you used your basketball-shooting skills to hit a shark on the nose with your basketball and scare it away ... but you would need to have a basketball with you when you were washed overboard, and it would only work for the first shark, unless you could swim very fast and retrieve the basketball before the second shark appeared. And if you could swim that fast, you'd be better off swimming very fast away from the sharks, rather than bopping them on the head with basketballs, which could annoy them.

So I don't totally object to swimming (because it can occasionally be useful) or cartwheeling (because it provides a different view of the world), but my general opinion is that most sport is fairly useless, and most sports-mad people are crazy.

Mallory was completely sports mad. That was only one reason not to like her. There were plenty more. I still hadn't found out which one of us was ahead on the name-count, but I was right about her liking to be in the centre of things.

On the other hand, I was wrong about her being a snake. The others were the snakes. She was the snake charmer, and she could make them do whatever she wanted.

Chapter Seven

"GOOD MORNING, EVERYONE. JESSICA, Mallory … if I can just interrupt your riveting conversation for a moment?"

I know about rivets. They're a sort of bolt for holding things together; Dad uses them in his workshop out in the garage. I watched Jessica and Mallory talking and laughing, and I could almost see them being pulled closer and closer, week by week, as the words coming out of their mouths riveted them together.

"Now then, let me guess. How many of you—"

No, I hadn't been inspired to find out any more about the endangered giant snail, and no, I hadn't talked to Mallory about it. Or about anything else.

Mr Cool was big on News. He said we ought to know what was going on in the world, but really he meant "the world of sport." Friday's News was just an excuse to talk about what games were being played over the weekend, and it was always boring. Monday's News was all about weekend sports results, and it was even more boring.

I whiled away the time drawing pictures of all the endangered animals listed on the board. I only half listened while Mr Cool reminded us that we needed to start thinking about our trip to the TV studios. He gave us a list of different roles, like reporter or news editor or weather presenter, and we had to write out a CV and apply for the one we wanted. I snoozed through Maths and hid at the back during Music.

But when the bell went for lunch, I didn't feel wildly enthusiastic about that, either. I still hung out with Jessica and the others, because that was the group I'd always hung out with. The difference was that I used to be in the middle of it, next to Jessica. Now Mallory had taken over, and I was somewhere on the outskirts.

Not that I ever wear skirts, because skirts are stupid. Perhaps that meant I was somewhere on the hem. One of those torn, raggedy hems you get on jeans when they are too long for you (or you're too short for them, which I always am, and Jessica never is).

Mallory's group was the loudest, and they always sounded as though they were having the most fun. They sat right in the middle of the playground, where everyone could see them. If there weren't any benches there, they pulled some up. Since Mallory arrived, her group had become the one that everyone aimed for. You could feel its magnetic pull from every corner of the school grounds.

There are other groups, but they're mostly dumb, or boring, or just plain weird. Or else they're boys, who make up one mass group of hooligans. The boys never bother about lunch, because they've eaten it all at morning break. They head straight down to the bottom field for an hour of bedlam, usually involving a ball, and occasionally a smashed window or a broken bone.

The girls in the sporty group get out netballs from the sports shed and shoot goals all lunchtime. The girls in the cellphone group pass round their phones to compare text messages and photos. I don't qualify for either group, even if I wanted to, because I can't shoot goals and

I don't have a cellphone.

Then there's the group that hangs out with the little kids, playing hide and seek, and lifting them off the climbing frames when they get stuck. One group reads in the library, and another group sits in one place and eats lunch very slowly while they talk about TV and boys. They can devote a whole hour to a pot of yoghurt and the latest episode of their favourite soap opera, or the newest song by their favourite boy band.

The MCAS group, clustered around Zoe, overlaps slightly with the TV-and-boys group, but they've written off most of the boys at school as being hopelessly immature. They try to catch Mr Cool's eye if he's on lunchtime duty, and argue over his favourite colour, food, café, music and movies. MCAS is supposed to be a secret society but Mr Cool is not stupid and I suspect he knows all about it.

Anyone left over makes up a small group of the permanently groupless. They're the ones nobody wants to hang out with; the ones with Special Needs teachers, or slightly odd clothes; the ones who never fit in anywhere. It's really a non-group, and nobody *ever* wants to be part of it.

So, I might have been shunted to the outer

edges of Mallory's group, but that still seemed a better option than being anywhere else.

Today there was the usual Monday conversation about the weekend's exciting events. As usual, I didn't have much to contribute. Then they started talking, *yet again,* about the Hawaiian Hula Hulas. I just don't get it about sports talk. Two teams play a game; one wins, the other loses. Or sometimes they draw. What else is there to say? I sighed heavily, thinking about months to come of boring indoor netball conversation.

"*What,* Harry?" Jessica said irritably.

I'd been wondering how a sigh could be heavy, when it's just made up of air. And how can you hold a breath, when you usually hold things in your hands ... or how can you *draw* a breath, for that matter? What would it look like? Now they were all looking at me, but at least I'd dragged their attention away from Mallory for once.

"Has your dad got a job yet?" Aleesha asked.

"No," I said. "But he's looking. He says something will turn up soon."

"Has your mum got one?" Piper asked.

"No. But she's looking, too."

"Bummer," Claudine said. "I'd hate to be poor."

"We're not *poor,*" I protested, and then I started

to wonder if maybe we were. Our money problems started when the building firm that Dad worked for went bust just before Christmas. The building industry was in a downturn, apparently, and Dad lost his job.

This mightn't have mattered so much except that Mum didn't have a job either. A few years ago, she took off her chef's hat, handed in her notice and went off to university. Some people thought she was crazy. I didn't, and Uncle Theo was on her side of course; although I did wish she'd chosen something more interesting to study. Like psychology. I could have read her psychology textbooks, which would have given me a deeper understanding of my teachers and classmates, and that could have proved very useful. But she chose law, and her textbooks had pages of law reports in small print, with rows of footnotes in even smaller print, which looked unbelievably boring. I didn't even try to read them.

"We're not *exactly* poor. Or only because of my Uncle Arthur," I told them. "He asked Dad for a loan after he lost everything in those bushfires. Dad transferred some money into his account over the Internet, but he didn't know Uncle Arthur had put a worm on our computer.

Uncle Arthur cleaned out our account and he's never been heard of since. He disappeared to Las Vegas."

"Was he on your Family Tree?" Claudine asked.

"Of course not. He's the black sheep of the family. You always leave them off," I said, although it did occur to me that if I ever had to do another Family Tree, it would be fun to decorate it with white sheep and black sheep.

"How do you know he went to Las Vegas, if he's never been heard of since?" Mallory asked.

Oops. I'd forgotten her father was a lawyer. After all, she only told us so about ten times a day. *Good one, Mallory. You think you have a smart legal brain, but ha ha to you.*

"A private investigator saw him there," I explained. "But that was the last sighting. Ever," I added, to underline the point. *Your father might be a lawyer, but I bet he's not a very good one.*

Jessica had never heard of my Uncle Arthur before (not surprising, seeing as he didn't exist). She looked very confused. So did the others, who had obviously forgotten about my wild imagination. But at least they'd noticed me, so I could feel I existed for a few minutes, until Mallory steered the conversation away again.

"How old d'you reckon those boys were that we played last week? High school age?"

Aleesha shook her head. "Nah, they were tall, but they acted too stupid to be at high school."

"Karl's tall," Claudine said.

"And he acts stupid," I pointed out.

"Who do you think's the most good-looking boy in our class?" Mallory said.

"Who cares?" I said, but they weren't listening.

"Who do *you* think?" Aleesha said.

Mallory considered for a while, although I reckoned she'd already decided, or she wouldn't have raised the subject. "Mmm – Karl, probably."

The other girls were all nodding. "He is good-looking," Piper agreed. "Even if he's a jerk most of the time. I like the way he does his hair."

I spluttered a bit. "Are we talking about the same boy? Karl Ballentyne looks as good as a football dragged through a cow-pat, and he doesn't do anything to his hair except empty a bottle of gel all over it."

"That's not what you *used* to think," Jessica said, looking slyly at the others.

"Oooh, Harry," someone said.

"What?" I said, glaring at Jessica. "You're

crazy. What are you talking about?" Luckily the bell rang.

"Yay, softball this afternoon!" Aleesha yelled, rushing off.

Softball is one of my least favourite sports, although it has a lot of competition for that spot. Whoever called it "soft" must have had a warped sense of humour, and the idea of anyone being excited about it stretched the limits of my imagination. (So your imagination isn't like a kite after all, or a wild animal; it's more like a length of elastic, or a TV ad for some home-gym equipment that you might do stretching exercises on, if you were stupid enough to buy it.)

For once, however, I was thankful for Room Nine's bizarre love of all sport, including softball, because it saved me from potential social humiliation when the other girls rushed off after Aleesha – all except me, Jessica and Mallory.

"*You* know," Jessica said, still looking sideways at Mallory and not at me. "Karl once wrote you a letter that said 'I love you Harry'."

"Jessica, he was four years old," I said. "We were at kindergarten. He couldn't even write properly. His mum had to help him with it. Come to think of it," I said, "he still can't write properly."

"See, you remember, though," Jessica said.

"Bet you've still got it somewhere. In your *special box,"* she said, grinning at Mallory.

Right. My box of special stuff that we used to go through once a year. *Secret* stuff, that we'd vowed we would never, ever tell *anyone* else about, and now Jessica had told Mallory, and soon it would be right round the class.

"Karl Ballentyne is a pizza-stuffing, pig-shooting, high-grade idiot," I said, fuming both at Jessica and at the idea that I would actually *like* someone who called me Harriet Weed Washington. The only thing that saved me was a sudden flash of inspiration: maybe Jessica only mentioned the letter to cover up the fact that she liked Karl herself.

"You'd better not tell anyone, that's all," I said, "or Karl will know it was you who told, Jessica. He'll sure know it wasn't me."

I saw Jessica trying to work out if that was true. "Yeah," she said reluctantly, "he probably would. Don't tell anyone, okay, Mallory?"

Mallory smiled her sly smile. "I won't," she said. "It can be our secret, ay, Jessica?"

I didn't care, really, if the whole class knew about four-year-old Karl's letter. That was ancient history, kindergarten stuff; it didn't mean anything. What I cared about was Jessica.

What was it with her these days? Not only did she not want to be my best friend any more, now she was lining up to be my worst enemy.

No – my second worst enemy. My all-time archenemy had to be evil Mallory Woz-Inky-Stinky-Bilinski.

Or whatever her stupid name was.

Chapter Eight

SOMEONE ONCE SAID THAT, IN THE FUTURE, everyone would be famous for fifteen minutes. A lot of kids in our class have already had their fifteen minutes and more.

Claudine is famous for swimming.

Jessica is famous for knowing the location of every clothes store in town, and being able to hold the greatest number of shopping bags in one hand.

Mr Cool is famous for his red sports car and shaving his hair off (although he's a teacher so it doesn't really count).

Karl is famous for the number of goals kicked in one match and the number of Cokes guzzled afterwards without throwing up. (As well as for the number of times he *did* throw up on the bus on the way to our school camp last year.)

Sadly, I will never get my fifteen minutes of fame for being tall, skinny and gorgeous-looking, like Jessica. I'm not sporty like Aleesha or Piper. I don't play any musical instruments like Callum, who is surprisingly good on drums and planning to be discovered on YouTube so he can be a world famous pop star by the time he's eighteen. My cakes sink and my biscuits turn out like concrete, so I'm not going to be the next TV MasterChef. I can't act, so I'm never going to be a famous movie star. I can't even sing, which is why I always hide down the back when we have music.

In our class, I am famous for a number of things, apart from my brilliantly creative projects, but they aren't necessarily things I *want* to be famous for. These are some of my claims to fame in Room Nine:

1. Having a lot of names.
2. Having wild and uncontrollable hair.
3. Losing things.

And you know what? None of them are my fault!

I can't be blamed for the wild hair. It's something I was born with – or, more precisely, something that grew on me. (In my baby photos I have no hair at all.) Mum wears her hair very short, but it's still full of tiny little curls, and in photos of her when she was younger you can see her hair flying all over the place, just like mine does. Uncle Theo used to have the uncontrollable Mabey hair too. He's gradually losing it, but what's left stands straight up as though it's trying to escape.

The name situation is certainly not my fault, seeing as I was only a few days old at the time, but I can't really blame Mum either. She and Dad planned to have a big family, only it didn't work out that way. They "tried and tried", Mum says (you don't want to think about that too much), but she couldn't get pregnant.

Finally, I turned up; so as well as 'Harriet', which was the name she and Dad liked best, she loaded me with all the other names she'd been saving up and might never get another chance to use. (And she was right, because she never did.) Her favourite flower: Jasmine. Favourite precious stone: Emerald. Favourite place-in-all-the-world: Florence, in Italy.

So that's me: Harriet Jasmine Emerald

Florence Mabey McDonald, which makes filling out forms a long and laborious business, but it could have been worse. A lot worse, as Karl Ballentyne frequently reminds me. 'Harriet Weed Washington' is only one of his not-so-helpful suggestions, which in the past have also included Harriet Cactus Coral, Harriet Topaz Timbuktu and Harriet Sphagnum Moss Seattle.

Imagine if Mum had included her favourite bird, or tree, or fruit? Favourite vegetable? (Harriet Artichoke Antarctica ... thanks Karl. Harriet Kiwifruit Kiwi ... yet another of his not-so-bright ideas.) Favourite superhero? Favourite filmstar? Just think about it. I try not to.

And at least you can't lose a name. However many you have, they trail along after the first one like ducklings after a mother duck, and you've got them for life. I manage to lose just about everything else. That's the third thing I'm famous for, and I'm sure that's not my fault either. Like the hair it's an inherited thing, because Mum and Uncle Theo are forever losing things: keys and wallets and pens, even memory sticks, which is kind of a joke, when you think about it. We need a memory stick embedded in our brains to tell us where we left things. That's a revolting thought, but it would be useful.

Mum once drove off with a pile of library books on the roof of the car, and she's terrible with keys. For Christmas one year, Dad bought her this beeper thing with an attachment to clip onto your key ring. The idea was that you could hit the beeper, and the key ring would beep back. The design flaw, of course, was that Mum kept losing the beeper.

Another time, she heard a programme on the radio that told you to vocalise what you were doing. She went round the house intoning, "I am putting my keys on the kitchen bench. I am putting my keys down beside the phone." But it didn't work. Mum was very good at remembering where she said she put the keys *the day before yesterday*, but not five minutes ago.

I tried it at school. "I am putting my pencil case in my desk. I am putting my lunch box on top of this shelf." But it didn't work for me either. All that happened was that the boys followed me round like robots, droning, "I am going crazy. I am losing my mind."

People who never lose stuff (like Dad) don't understand this, but things just vanish. They disappear. One moment I'm holding them, and the next moment they're gone. A good reason for not getting me a cellphone, Dad says, although that's just an excuse. His own phone is the oldest, clunkiest one possible; they don't even make phones like that any more. But it's all related to the building downturn: no money to upgrade it, and certainly no money to buy a phone for me (which is the real reason I don't have one, rather than the probability that I would lose it as soon as I got it).

Personally, I think the reason I lose things is because my mind is so full of other stuff, that the bit about "where did I put my wallet?" (or in Mum's case "my keys", and in Uncle Theo's case "my lecture notes") gets shunted out by more interesting and imaginative ideas, such as my non-existent Uncle Arthur. One day I might go to university myself and take psychology, just so I can test my theory out.

You can lose stuff. Keys, homework, drink bottles, pencil sharpeners. The piece of paper you were holding a second ago. The important school notice that's due back tomorrow. You can lose your voice, or your temper. You can lose track of time, like when you're absorbed in a book or a drawing, but that's not necessarily a bad thing. You can lose games, but that's kind of different, because they don't matter, and you never had them to start with. You can lose your way, but that only counts if you knew where you were going in the first place. You can lose your hair, so you wouldn't need to worry about losing your comb or hairbrush, but then you'd probably lose your cap or beanie instead. You can lose your driver's licence. You can lose money, or your job.

I always thought you couldn't lose friends, but obviously I was wrong about that. You can, in fact, be a total loser, and that was pretty much me, this year.

One thing I have decided lately is that I don't like change. I wish you could choose a time when everything is going well and freeze it, so you could stay there forever; or at least for a year or two, and then you could fast-forward and skip the bad bits in between.

Obviously, there would be problems to iron out. For example, Karl Ballentyne would want to freeze his kindergarten time-frame *before* I fell off the bars and they closed the playground, whereas I would be quite happy to freeze it *afterwards*, when we all got to stay inside and play with paint and play dough. Perhaps you would need a lot of parallel universes to make it work; but if I could, I would have frozen my personal time-frame before this year even started.

The summer holidays were long, hot and

boring. Everyone else was away, but Dad had just lost his job and we didn't have the money to go anywhere. Mum (finally qualified, after years of listening to boring lectures and reading boring textbooks) spent most of her time poring over job ads or going to interviews (but not getting the job). Dad spent most of his time slumped in front of the TV, watching mindless hours of mindless cricket.

Jessica went off to her family's beach house. Other years, she'd invited me to come and stay for a weekend, or even a whole week, and I'd hoped she might ask me again, but she didn't. Instead she came back at the end of the holidays, all tanned and another few centimetres taller, and told me about the fabulous time she'd had and all the hot boys that had been at the beach this year. Maybe that was why she didn't ask me to come. Hot boys wouldn't look twice at me, but they would swarm around Jessica like bees round a hive. Jessica must've thought that I'd just cramp her style.

I had even looked forward to going back to school, things were that bad ... but look what happened! I was trapped in a class of sports freaks, my best friend had abandoned me, Mallory Woz-Jerk-Slinki treated me like dirt, and nobody else was particularly interested in me, except for one girl who didn't even speak English properly.

It wasn't meant to be like this. Year Eight was *meant* to be our best year. We were top of the school at last! Role models! All the little kids looked up to us. They even looked up to boys like Karl Ballentyne, who was the total opposite of a role model!

We got to do all the cool stuff, like the trip to the TV studios, and all the other stuff like buddy classes, Leadership teams and Workplace Interviews (that might not be quite so cool, but did give you time off school work). And everything would be leading up to the ultra-exciting (even though we were all way too cool to admit it) Leaving Dinner, and the big dilemma about which boy you were taking to the End-of-Year Dance. (This was mainly a dilemma for the girls, because sometimes the boys didn't even know that they'd been taken, but it was still important to decide.)

But it wasn't working out that way. Everything was different. The classes had got all jumbled up, Jessica had got taller and I hadn't. And then Mallory Ridiculous-Surname Woz-Nick-Jetski turned up, and things got worse.

Chapter Nine

LIFE WAS NOT TOTAL DOOM AND GLOOM. There was always Uncle Theo: Mum's older brother, and one of my favourite people. Dad liked him too, "just a pity about all those blimmin' cats," he always added.

Uncle Theo had no kids of his own, and he was very generous with money at Christmas and birthdays. I was pinning my hopes on him rescuing us from starvation if our money ran out before Mum or Dad managed to get a job. He could keep us in groceries, if we promised not to splurge on anything fancy, or too much chocolate.

Another good thing about Uncle Theo was

that he loved cats. People handed their cats over to him if they were going overseas, or if they found a stray, or had a kitten they couldn't get rid of, and he could never say no. You either love cats or you don't, and non-cat-lovers don't get it, but there's something mysterious, almost magical, about them. If you *really* look at a cat – its whiskers, the way it swishes and whisks its tail, the sharp claws that slide in and out of their sheaths, the markings on its coat, the way it scrambles up trees and balances on ledges, its intent look when it stalks birds and mice – it's as if a wild animal, cousin to a tiger or a cheetah, has walked out of the jungle and into your house.

I suppose this is another Mabey thing, and I should have put it down as number 4 on the list of things I am nearly famous for: being animal crazy. Unfortunately, animal-craziness is not shared by the McDonald side of the family.

For a long time, we didn't have pets because of Dad. I never wanted a baby brother or sister, but I always wanted a pet. I walked other people's dogs (even though carrying a plastic bag makes you look stupid, and it's even more embarrassing if you have to use it). I looked after the neighbours' cats when their owners went on holiday, and sometimes I stuck travel brochures in their letterboxes, to try and encourage them to go away more often.

Jessica has a cat, a rabbit and two guinea pigs, which she only used to notice when I visited. The rabbit was called Bunny; not a very imaginative name, but that's not surprising as Jessica doesn't have much of an imagination. It was fed up with being hugged and squashed by her little brothers, so it could be grumpy and twitchy, but it let me cuddle it, and the two guinea pigs would squeak when I picked them up. Not in an excited, Zoe-Watson sort of way, but in a contented, happy-guinea-pig sort of way.

But it was different for Dad. Cats that waited on walls and fences, and purred when I stroked them, leapt off as soon as he approached. Dogs wagged their tails at me but barked at him. If he called round to Jessica's place – back in the days when I still went there – the guinea pig snuggled in my arms would scramble away to a corner of its cage.

He and animals didn't have a good relationship. They didn't have any sort of relationship. They just didn't get on, even though Dad loved Mum and Mum loved animals, so you would think – logically speaking – that Dad should, too. It should work out like a mathematical equation, but it didn't. I suppose people aren't all that logical.

Uncle Theo loved his cats but, being forgetful, he sometimes forgot that they needed to eat. We would go round to visit him, and find all the cats waiting patiently by their empty food bowls. He kept running out of cat food because he'd forget to buy any more, and once he forgot about the cats completely. Our phone went in the middle of the night and it was Uncle Theo calling from Belfast in Ireland, asking if we could go round and feed them for the next two weeks!

This makes him sound like a stereotypical absent-minded professor, which is exactly what he is. Maybe not all professors are like that, but I think Philosophy ones (like him) must be, because they are buried so deep in their philosophical thoughts. I've often thought it'd be fun to hide and watch him and all the other absent-minded professors bumping into each other in the university corridors as they forget where they're going or what they're supposed to be doing. It would be like one of those nature programmes about the undersea world, where you see fish cruising along, bumping into each other and then shooting off in another direction.

But on the whole, the cats managed, and Uncle Theo managed ... until he won a scholarship to go overseas for six months. Uncle Theo specialised in something very obscure, so he loved it when he could go and visit other professors working in the same field, and they could talk about it together and actually understand each other. Of course they didn't really work in a field, although when Uncle Theo got absorbed in something he would look as though he didn't quite know where he was, so probably a field would work just as well as an office, unless it was raining.

Uncle Theo didn't think his cats would like being in a cattery for all that time, and it would have cost a lot, so in the end it made sense for them to come to us. We went from having no pets to seven of them: Cleo, Polly, Oscar, Alfie, Lucy, Max and Tilda. It made perfect sense to Mum, to me and to Uncle Theo – just not to Dad.

"Great help, thanks, Em," Uncle Theo said, as we collected the cats a week before he was due to leave. "Appreciate it, Jack, especially given your anti-feline predilections."

Em (short for Emily) is my mum. Jack is my dad. His name isn't short for anything, so it suits him because he's not exactly tall (like me) but with him, that never seems to matter. I think it's because he's so good with his hands, so clever at fixing things that are broken, that he makes you feel everything will work, just because he's there.

Everything ... apart from living in a houseful of cats.

"Come on, Dad. It won't be that bad," I tried to reassure him as we let the cats out of their travelling boxes. The house was full of their mewing as they started to explore.

"Wanna bet?" Dad said. "It's all right for you, Harry. You *like* cats, but the idea of having all those animals in the house makes my flesh creep."

"Mum and I will look after them. You won't have to do anything," I said, but the idea of Dad's flesh creeping made mine creep too. What did flesh look like when it crept? Where did it creep to? Would you see all the blood and stuff underneath? *Yuck!*

There went my imagination again – zooming away on a blood-streaked course of its own.

Chapter Ten

ON SATURDAY MORNINGS I USUALLY MESS about and relax, because I don't waste them by playing sport, although occasionally I have to spoil them with homework. Like this Saturday.

I wanted to fuss over Uncle Theo's cats, and help them to settle into their new living space, but instead I was meant to be transforming a blank sheet of paper into my CV for our trip to the TV studios. Creating my CV was another thing that I had been putting off, like talking to Mallory about our Conservation topic.

The problem was that I wanted to be a newsreader. That was the best job, and the most fun, and at the beginning of the year Jessica and I had planned to apply together. She would provide the glamour, and I would provide the ability to read from a cue card. We were going to think up a name for our dream newsreader team – or *I* was going to think up a name – but that hadn't happened. I couldn't think of a name, and I wasn't even sure if Jessica wanted to be part of our team any more. Should I ask her? Or should I just go ahead and apply on my own? What if Jessica had teamed up with someone else? Would she do that without telling me?

I didn't know much about CVs but I knew they started with your name and contact details at the top. Name, address, cellphone number (*if only!*), followed by previous work experience, interests and referees.

Name: Harriet Jasmine Emerald Florence Mabey McDonald

Did that look like the name of a top newsreader? Or did it just look ridiculous? *Good evening. Here is the latest news, with Harriet Jasmine Emerald Florence Mabey McDonald.* It would be time for the weather before I'd even finished giving my name! Mind you, it probably ruled out being a reporter too, which had been my second choice. *Now we'll cross to our reporter in the field,*

Harriet Jasmine Emerald – who? – Florence – where?

Polly leapt onto my knee and sat there, purring like an engine. She's a British blue, with soft, grey fur, leathery-looking ears, and a coat so smooth that your fingers slide over it, like running your hand over cold starlight. Uncle Theo got her from someone at work, who was moving to Australia. I rubbed her back, and she purred even louder.

"You should feel how soft and silky she is, Dad."

"Yes, I'm sure." Dad edged past with a mug of coffee and a handful of chocolate biscuits. He sat down on the sofa with one arm flung over the side, drumming his fingers until Tilda, the little tabby kitten, pounced on them.

"Blimmin' cats!" Dad said under his breath, snatching his hand away.

"It's not her fault," I said. "She thought you were playing a game with her."

"Well, I wasn't," Dad said crossly. "I don't play games with cats. They should have figured that out by now."

More cats prowled around the floor, tails waving, or pressed against our legs. Tilda climbed into an empty box and peered out with big eyes. The brown Burmese leapt up onto the back of the sofa and settled itself behind Dad's head.

"Isn't it funny how they don't seem to know you don't like them," I said.

"They do know," Dad growled. "They're doing it on purpose."

"If it says full name, do you *have* to put your full name?" I asked Mum when she arrived home from the gym, her face glowing and her hair smelling of her favourite raspberry shampoo. Minutes later, the front doorbell rang and there was Uncle Theo, leaning his bike up against the wall, with a wide smile on his face.

"Harry! Em! Jack! Good to see you," he said.

Uncle Theo was leaving the next day, and he'd come round to borrow a suitcase. Mum poured more coffee. Polly hopped off my lap and settled herself on Uncle Theo's, purring so loudly that she sounded like a small plane about to take off. The tabby kitten launched herself at Dad's (luckily empty) coffee mug and knocked it over.

"Tilda, you ridiculous juvenile!" Uncle Theo said. "I must apologise for her, she's extremely scatty. So, Jack, how's your employment search going?"

"It's not," Dad said. "But something's bound to turn up soon." He sounded quite cheerful.

I thought he ought to be panicking a bit more, personally, but that's what he kept telling everyone: that something would turn up soon.

"I hope so," Mum sighed. She didn't sound nearly so cheerful. "Plenty of job ads, but I'm too old. They all want someone younger."

"You're not old, Mum," I protested. "You're not even the oldest parents in my class. Jessica's parents, now *they're* old," I said, before I remembered that I wasn't best friends with Jessica now, so her parents no longer mattered.

"I am for these law firms," Mum said. "You should see them, all glass doors and expensive furniture, and everyone wearing designer outfits, and stick-thin."

Uncle Theo and I exchanged glances. What were we supposed to say to that? Mum's favourite outfits are casual, not designer, and she goes to the gym regularly but she's not *stick-thin*. I wouldn't want her to be, either; it sounds very uncomfortable. Who wants to be hugged by a stick?

"How do you think your dad will cope with this feline invasion?" Uncle Theo murmured as he got ready to go. The cats twined round his legs, not wanting him to leave.

"He'll be fine," I said. "They're all nice cats."

"Keep an eye on him while I'm away," Uncle

Theo said. "Look after your mother, and most importantly, look after yourself."

"I will," I promised. But I didn't want him to leave either. I was missing him already, and he hadn't even left the country.

We had to take Uncle Theo and his bike back to his place because he'd got a puncture and had forgotten his puncture kit, plus he'd forgotten that the suitcase wouldn't fit on the back of the bike anyway! It didn't look like he'd done much packing, even though he was leaving in less than twenty-four hours, but at least he'd remembered that he needed a suitcase, so that was something.

We drove back home, Dad parked on the road outside, and he and Mum got out. I was about to, when I saw Jessica race out of their gate, five or six houses further down. Her hair swung out as she went, and she flipped it back with one hand. Jessica's hair always does exactly what it's supposed to. If it's tied up, it stays tied up, because it's long and silky instead of wild and frizzy, and because she puts lots of fancy clips in it, which I can never be bothered with ... and anyway, I lose them all.

Mum stuck her head back through the window.

"There's Jessica," she said brightly. "Hasn't she got taller lately?"

Yes, she had. I hadn't, because my clothes and shoes still fitted, and I knew I wouldn't get any new ones until I'd grown out of them. It felt like I'd been wearing the same old trackpants and jeans for most of my life.

"Is she coming over, do you think?" Mum said.

"Doubt it," I muttered.

Did Jessica look like someone who wanted to be part of a dream newsreader team with me? Doubt it.

Mum and Dad hadn't cottoned on to the fact that we weren't best friends any more. They hadn't noticed that we didn't walk to school together, or that Jessica hadn't been round to our place for weeks. It wasn't their fault. I knew they were preoccupied by other things, like the building downturn, Dad not having a job, and whether Mum would find one before our money ran out.

And whose fault was it, anyway, that we'd stopped being best friends? Was it her fault, or mine? Was it Evil Mallory Woz-Think-I'm-A-Whiz-Ski's? Or was it the fault of those extra centimetres that she'd put on, not just in height, but all over?

Hard to say. But I waited till she was gone – and she kept her eyes straight ahead, too, as she ran past, wallet in one hand, brand new cellphone in the other – before I got out of the car.

Chapter Eleven

THE OLD COUPLE WHO LIVED NEXT DOOR to us had just sold up and moved out. They used to screech at you if you trod on a centimetre of their front lawn, so I wasn't sorry they'd gone, and I'd already built up a mental picture of the new family. There would be a boy at high school, who was extremely good-looking, and Jessica would have her eye on him straightaway but he'd like me better because we were neighbours. And he would have a sister almost exactly my age, in fact our birthdays would only be a few days apart, and she would hate shopping and sport, so we could hang out together nearly all the time.

On Saturday afternoon, Mum went over to say hello, taking new-neighbour gifts of blueberry muffins and flowers. She came back and reported that they did have two kids, a boy and a girl. But sadly, the boy was about my age, and the girl was younger.

That didn't sound like much of an improvement on the Screechers. A boy my age, who would be a pain like Karl, and a younger sister, who would whine and be annoying. I wiped my mental picture from my mental whiteboard, and didn't bother to redraw it.

Uncle Theo doesn't have a car, because he bikes or walks everywhere, so on Sunday morning Dad went to pick him up. They called in briefly so Uncle Theo could say a last goodbye to the cats and to us, but he didn't want Mum or me to come to the airport with them, which was just as well, because I hate airport goodbyes. "See you in six months!" he called, and then he was gone, waving out the window as they turned the corner.

"Did he get away all right?" Mum asked when Dad got back. "Did he remember his passport? And his tickets?"

"Hope so," Dad said. He felt round for the remote and slumped down on the sofa, then leapt up as if he'd been zapped. "That blasted cat! Why does Theo have to go in for animals that match the furniture?"

The brown Burmese shot off the sofa and went hurtling through the kitchen as though a pack of wild dogs was chasing him.

"Max. His name's Max," I said, but Dad never bothered to remember the cats' names. He called them all the same thing: *that blimmin' cat!* Unless he was feeling extra stressed, when it was, *that blasted cat!* Or, if there were more than one of them, *those blasted cats!*

The cats probably have a name for Dad, too, and I bet it's much the same, except they say *man* instead of *cat*.

Our house is not very big, and my bedroom is so small that I can almost touch all four walls when I'm lying in bed. It only just fits a bed, a chest of drawers and a bookcase, but that's okay because there's less space to lose things in, although it's amazing how often you can lose something even in a small space.

My bookcase is full of all the best animal stories ever written. All the classics, like *Dr Dolittle* and *Black Beauty,* and several books by Mum's and my favourite author, Connor O'Connor, which I would have lots of time to read now that Jessica and I weren't doing anything together, and there wasn't a girl next door with almost the same birthday as me to hang out with. My walls were plastered with pictures from animal calendars that Mum and Dad gave me every Christmas. Some of those pictures had been up for years and, to tell the truth, I was getting a bit sick of them but I didn't have anything to replace them with.

However, I'd never had real, live animals in my room before, apart from hopeful spiders or lost bumblebees or the occasional mouse. Now Tilda slept on my bed all night, and pounced on my toes whenever I rolled over. Alfie rubbed up against my legs, and Polly purred on my knee while I ate breakfast and wondered where Uncle Theo was: still on the plane? Booking into a hotel? Was he having breakfast too, or was he in a totally different time zone by now?

Dad raised a hand in farewell from where he was sprawled on the sofa in the lounge, eating toast and watching breakfast TV.

"Bye, Harry," Mum called. "Have a good day at school." *Not much chance of that.* "Oof! Get out of here!" she exclaimed, tripping over Max again.

A white van reversed down the next-door

driveway as I shut the front door. *J. Buckler Electrical* it said on the side. A boy was coming down the path with a book in his hand, and several more sticking out of his backpack. The first thing I noticed – apart from how heavy his book looked, in both senses – was the brown hair that flopped over his forehead, rather than being all gelled up like Karl Ballentyne's.

The second thing I noticed was that he was at least a head taller than me, although it was hard to tell because his head was bent over the book, and anyway, I've always thought that's an odd sort of measurement. If someone is a head shorter or taller than someone else, it sounds like one of them has no head. If they're half a head shorter, you start thinking about a head sliced in half with all the brains oozing out of it (*yuck*) which is worse than thinking about pig hunting or flesh creeping.

This illustrates one of the drawbacks of a wild imagination. You don't always know what it's going to throw up, and sometimes you're presented with images that you'd rather not have wildly imagined.

Anyway, this boy was taller than me, but he did have a head, and it wasn't cut in half. Still reading, he fumbled to open their front gate.

Behind him, a girl in a St Benedict's uniform was waving to the van as it drove away tooting. She saw me, dodged past the boy and burst out talking as soon as she got close enough.

"Hello! You're Harriet, aren't you?"

"Just Harry." (I wasn't going into the whole Jasmine Emerald Florence thing.)

"I'm Ellie, and that's Adam, the one with his nose in a book who can't hear us."

Adam slowed to a halt. He leaned back against the fence, turned a page and waved without lifting his eyes.

"You don't go to St Benedict's, do you? Which school do you go to? North Park?" I nodded again. "Our mum's a child minder and I have to help sometimes," Ellie went on, hardly pausing for breath. "She looks after twins and a baby. Our dad's an electrician, but I think child minding is much more stressful. You can turn electricity off, but you can't turn children off."

"She doesn't want to know all that, Ellie," the boy called Adam said, turning another page.

"Yes, she does. I bet it's way more interesting than what you're reading. What's it about, anyway?"

"The history of mathematics," he said, without looking up. "Pythagoras."

"See?" Ellie said. "Have you got a cellphone?" she asked.

"No," I said.

"Me neither," Ellie said sadly.

"Not old enough," her brother said.

"It's not a matter of age. It's a matter of social invisibility, and being left out of social networks," Ellie said grandly.

Social invisibility. I knew all about that. Ellie changed tack again. If she'd been changing tack in a sailing boat, she'd have been zigzagging all over the harbour by now.

"You've got amazing hair," she said. "You've got the reddest, curliest hair I ever saw in my whole life. It's so frizzy, it's as frizzy as a fabulous flying fox."

"Being rude, Ellie," Adam said into his book.

"I'm not being rude. It was a compliment," Ellie said. "I wish I had hair like that. What happens when you get nits?"

"I don't get nits," I said, with dignity.

"Lucky. You wouldn't be able to get them out once they got in. Do you really not get them? I do. I thought everyone did."

"Too much information," Adam said.

"No, it isn't," Ellie said. "I'm just stating a fact. You like facts."

"Do you go to St Benedict's too?" I asked Adam, because he wasn't in uniform.

"He's home-schooled," Ellie informed me. "Coz he's smarter than all the teachers and he gets bored in class. But Mum doesn't have time to teach him, so he teaches himself, mostly. Mum says he ought to go to high school but he thinks he'll hate it, so she makes him practise sometimes at our school, but he just goes to the library. See you later," she called cheerfully, and skipped off singing a little song.

"Cleo," the boy said, shifting his gaze from his book to somewhere around knee-level. The first thing he'd said to me, and he'd got my name wrong.

"I'm Harry," I said.

"I know," the boy said. "That's Cleo." He gestured at the Siamese cat that was winding round his legs, obviously pleased to see him. "Your mum told me all their names. She must be Cleo. Siamese cats are usually friendly and inquisitive."

Cleo obviously didn't know that, because she was never very friendly with people she didn't know, but right now she was yowling in a loud, ecstatic, totally-Siamese sort of way. Adam bent down to pat her. When he looked up at last, his eyes and Cleo's were identically blue and clear.

I almost expected Cleo to open her mouth and speak as well, but she didn't, of course, and he didn't say anything else.

"Come on, Adam," Ellie called from further down the street. He turned another page and followed her, still reading, and somehow avoiding any lampposts or bushes in the way. Maybe he'd developed some special way of detecting obstacles without looking.

"Bye," I said, but he didn't answer.

I turned and went the other way, towards Jessica's place. She swung out of her gate, yelling, "Hurry up slow coach!" and we set off to school together, talking our heads off, although not really, because you couldn't talk once your head had fallen off . . .

You know what?

That didn't happen.

I did see Jessica up ahead, so I walked very slowly, which made the walk even longer and more boring than usual. But I didn't want to catch up with her until we got to school, where there would be lots of other people around, and it wouldn't be so noticeable that we weren't talking to each other.

Jessica and I *used* to walk to school together. Whoever was ready first (usually me, because she spent so long doing her hair and choosing her outfit for the day) always waited for the other one.

It wasn't that I didn't *want* to talk to her. We just didn't have much to say. The things she talked about, I wasn't interested in; like whether she should buy this top or that skirt, or both, and when the next issue of her favourite magazine was due out, and why it wasn't fair that her dad wouldn't buy her a new cellphone when her last one was like, so out of date. And she didn't seem interested in the cats, or where Uncle Theo was going, or whether Dad would get a job before we starved to death.

Oops. I'd forgotten about having to pass the shops. Jessica and Mallory often came down to buy stuff before school, even though you weren't meant to. They were coming out now, laughing, and carrying packets of chips and cans of drink.

"Like my new earrings?" Jessica said to her, turning her head to show them off.

"Are they the ones you bought on Saturday?" Mallory asked. "Yeah, they're cool."

I hate shopping. It's so boring. But Jessica *always* goes into town in the weekends. She has a monthly allowance, which she spends in the first week, and then she nags and nags until her mother gives her some more to tide her over till the next month.

"You know that top I bought?" Jessica said.

"The yellow one?" Mallory said. "It looked great on you."

Mallory's already seen the new top, said my private-detective brain. *So either they've been shopping together, or one of them has been round to the other one's place.*

"Nah," Jessica said, "I've gone off it. I might take it back if I can be bothered, or I'll give it to someone. Maybe I'll swap it for something with my sister."

I know they saw me. They were right in front of me, only metres away. But they kept on talking and totally ignored me. They didn't even say hello.

So I did. I still don't like being ignored, even though it's been happening all year. "Hello," I called, waving my arms around. "Harry to Jessica, hello, hello."

"What? Who's that?" Jessica said, making out she hadn't seen me, or maybe she was pretending that there was more than one idiot standing there waving her arms around. "Oh, it's you. Hi, Harry." And then she went right back to her conversation with Mallory as though I was just a nobody.

I am not a nobody. I am me. I am Harriet Jasmine Emerald Florence Mabey McDonald. But who really cares? Who cares if Jessica and I have been friends for years, and now we're not? Who cares if we went to the same kindergarten, started school within a week of each other and have been in the same class ever since? Who cares if we've planned every birthday party together since we turned five, told each other all our deepest darkest secrets and had sleepovers at each other's houses almost every weekend? Who cares if she's been taken over by Do-It-My-Way Mallory Woz-Know-It-All-Ski?

I don't. I don't care.

Yes, I do. I can't help it. I do care.

Chapter Twelve

"GOOD MORNING, ROOM NINE," MR COOL said. "How many of you—"

"Morning, Mr Cameron," Zoe called out. "Nice shirt."

"Thanks, Zoe," Mr Cool said. "Any comments on the tie before we get started?"

"The tie's good, too," Zoe said. "Did Carmen buy that one for you?"

"No, she didn't," Mr Cool said. "Can I go on now? Thank you. As I was saying, how many of you did some work on your projects over the weekend?"

No, I didn't. There was no way I was going to waste even a minute of my weekend talking to Mallory Woz-Nik-Nak-Nutski.

Zoe wasn't listening, because she was too busy exchanging significant glances with the other MCAS members. They would be saving up this new development to discuss at lunchtime: Did the tie situation mean that Mr Cool and Carmen had broken up?

Nobody answered, because nobody had done any work on anything over the weekend, except sport or shopping, not that you could call either of them 'work'.

"Yeah, well, I couldn't," Karl said. "Soccer, see."

Our class is so predictable. Following the usual pattern of our (un)exciting Monday mornings, there would be News to start with, which meant more weekend sporting results, and would be boring. Maths, which was bearable. Music. And after lunch, Sport. What could be worse than that?

Sometimes we have a whole afternoon of Art. I love Art, but even that doesn't make up for having to spend a whole day at school.

But still, who really cared? Not me. Whatever happened at school, at least I could go back home to the cats, and *nothing* could be better than that. I loved having Uncle Theo's cats around all day, and finding the warm weight of one of them on my bed in the middle of the night. I loved waking up and hearing a funny clicking noise, which was Alfie, who liked sleeping on the computer keyboard, and kneaded the keys as he slept.

I loved feeding the cats and looking after them. I could happily spend all day thinking about going home again. For a cat-lover who had never been allowed a pet before, it was pure bliss. I sat at my desk and recited their names to myself: *Polly, Max, Cleo, Tilda, Oscar, Alfie, Lucy* ... Or alphabetically: *Alfie, Cleo, Lucy, Max, Oscar, Polly, Tilda* ...

"Harry! Are you listening to me?"

"Yes, Mr C— Mr Cameron," I said, snapping to. But a few minutes later I was off again, not daydreaming about the cats this time, but worrying about Uncle Theo. Last time he went overseas, he got pickpocketed on a bus in Rome and left his jacket on a train in Paris. I knew how easily he could lose his passport or his tickets, or simply forget where he was going. What was he doing, right now? Hanging out at some foreign airport? Ordering strange food from menus written in strange-looking scripts? Tapping away on his laptop, trying to find the email that told him what country he was meant to be in?

"Harry!" Mr Cool's voice seemed to come from a long way away. There was a burst of giggling, but I didn't look round. I knew who it would be. "Are you with us today?"

"Yes, right here," I said. "Extremely present."

"And sometimes correct," Mr Cool said, with a smile that was guaranteed to make MCAS members keel over. "Can you tell me what we're doing right now?"

"Um ... maths?" I guessed.

"Right. Surveys. Art on Thursdays, remember?"

"Yes, sure," I said, surprised.

"So—" Mr Cool gestured at my refill pad. I looked down and saw it was covered with cat doodles. Cats stretching and jumping and climbing, or curled up asleep. Two or three of them were thin and elegant with pointed faces, just like Cleo, and they were ...

"I'll take that for now, shall I?" Mr Cool said, ripping off the top sheet. "You can have it back when the bell goes." He folded up the drawing and slid it into his pocket.

I worked very hard at maths for the rest of the lesson, trying not to be noticed. We were meant to be doing surveys and then tabulating and graphing the results. Everyone else had chosen boring and totally predictable questions, like "What is your favourite clothes brand?" (Jessica, and she didn't even have an option for "don't know" or "don't care") or "What is your favourite sport?" (Karl Ballentyne, ditto). Mallory wanted to do "Who is your favourite teacher at this school?" or, even better, "Who is your least favourite teacher?" but sadly, Mr Cool said no.

I still couldn't stand Mallory Woz-Whatever-ski, but I had to admit that she did come up with some good ideas. That made her sound like a fish, diving down to the ocean floor and surfacing again with some undersea treasure. If she were a fish, I bet she'd be one of those long, thin, slippery ones with mean-looking, pointed snouts. I'd be something bright and tropical, with stripes.

My idea was the best, as usual. I'd once read an article about changing trends in pet names, and how cats and dogs nowadays are given much more human-sounding names than they used to be. The article said nobody called their pets "Smokey" or "Blackie" or "Lucky" any more. They were more likely to give them a real name, like Holly, or Molly, or Polly. So I went round the whole school, asking everyone what their cats and dogs were called.

Most kids just surveyed the others in our class, but I asked everyone, even the teachers, and the caretaker, and Esther in the office, and Mac who fixes the computers when they stuff up. It took ages, because I also had to listen to all their pet stories: why they weren't allowed to have one (some of the little kids cried at this point), or why they wouldn't want one (that was only Karl Ballentyne, so it didn't count) or why they chose that particular name and all the clever things their dog or cat had ever done.

It also took a long time to count up the names, and write them out in fancy scripts, and decorate the margins with pictures of cats and dogs. Plus, I lost a whole batch of answers. I turned my desk upside down, literally, trying to find them, but I couldn't, so I had to go back and ask two classes all over again.

"Harry," Mr Cool said, "you do realise, don't you, that nearly everyone has finished their graphs, and you haven't even started yours?"

"Yes," I said. *But so what? Drawing graphs is easy. Anyone can draw graphs.* (I didn't say that out loud, though. I was still trying not to be noticed.)

The principal came in just after that to ask Mr Cool about something, and he did his usual cruise around, because he likes to think he's In Touch with What's Happening In Today's Classrooms. He checked out a few of the other graphs and pointed out mistakes.

Then he stopped at my desk and stood there for a while, without saying anything. I could tell Mr Cool was watching. I knew he was hoping Mr Bennett would point out the fact that I hadn't started my graph yet.

"You didn't ask *me*," Mr Bennett said at last. "*My* cat is called Lucky."

"Great," I said, writing it in. "*Lucky* I hadn't started my graph yet."

Mr Cool made that noise at the back of his throat that sounded suspiciously like *Grrrr*!

"Go on with your work, everyone. Thanks for that, Mr Cameron," the principal called out.

"She's a nice cat, that Lucky," I heard him muttering as he headed out the door. "Maybe it's time I got another one to keep her company. Not another black one, though – a grey one would be nice. Lucky and Smokey, that sounds like a good match."

Chapter Thirteen

I HOPED MR COOL MIGHT FORGET ABOUT the drawing that he had slid into his pocket, and the paper would go through the wash with his trousers and it would all get washed away.

When the bell finally went, I thought I would just slide away, too.

"Harry," Mr Cool said, as I was attempting to slide through the door.

I still half-hoped that he'd forgotten, and he was just going to have another go at me about my non-existent graph. But he hadn't, of course. I have to admit that Mr Cool is not only super-cool, he's super-smart as well.

He unfolded the drawing and spread it out on

his desk. Zoe and a cluster of MCAS girls, the ones who always try to be last out of the classroom, were lurking and giggling by the door. "Off you go," he said, without looking up. They giggled some more and retreated.

Impressive, I thought. *Seeing out of the corner of his eye, when his eye doesn't even have any corners.*

Mr Cool stood there and contemplated my drawing. "Want to tell me about it, Harry?" he said.

"Uh – well, they're just cats, that's all," I said.

Mr Cool looked quizzical. That was a good word and it was exactly how he looked, his eyebrows jumping up and down like z's on his forehead. The longer I talked, the longer I didn't have to be hanging around on the raggedy hem of Mallory's group outside. "See, we're looking after all these cats for my uncle, while he's away, and this one is like Oscar, who sleeps all the time, and this one is like Cleo who's a Siamese, and—"

"And this one?" said Mr Cool. He wasn't pointing at a cat. He was pointing at an open-mouthed, round-eyed figure waving her arms about, who was being buried under an onslaught of sharp-clawed Cleo clones. A bubble coming out of the figure's mouth said: "*Help! My Roxy™ handbag!*"

"I put the trademark sign in," I said. "It's quite legal."

Mr Cool looked at me. Then he looked back at the picture. "I might be wrong," he mused, "but this figure looks to me quite a lot like Mallory."

"Does it?" I said. "That's a coincidence."

"Isn't it?" Mr Cool said. He looked over my head thoughtfully, tapping a pencil against his teeth and not saying anything for a while. A nice, sharp pencil. "You know, it can be hard starting at a new school," he said at last, as though we were talking about something completely different.

"Really?" I said politely. I thought about asking if he was speaking from personal experience, but that might have been taking things just a bit too far.

Mr Cool looked at me again, as though he knew I knew what he meant. "Sometimes it takes a while to work out who you really want to be friends with."

This time, I didn't say anything.

"How are you and Mallory getting on with your Conservation project?"

"Fine," I said.

"Well, if there's ever anything you want to talk to me about, Harry ..."

There were quite a few things, actually, like why we couldn't have more Art and less Maths, why we had to have Sport at all and why assembly couldn't be made a whole lot shorter, maybe by telling the principal that he couldn't attend, but I didn't think that was quite what he had in mind.

"Sure," I said. "Can I go now?"

"Sure," Mr Cool said. As I headed for the door, he said, "Oh, Harry—" He was holding out my drawing. "You know, you have a vivid imagination, and you also have the talent to give it full expression. Which may or may not always be a good thing."

"Uh ... thanks," I said, stuffing the picture into my pocket, and wondering if that was a compliment or not.

"Because sometimes," Mr Cool said, "just occasionally, you might need to curb your imagination a little bit." He put on his quizzical, eyebrow-jumping look again, while I was wondering what the speed limit for the imagination would be, and whether you could get a ticket for going over it.

Then I started thinking about those road

signs with exclamation marks that warn you to *Slow down! Roadworks ahead.* Perhaps that's what I need. My own personal road sign, warning everyone *Danger! Imagination at work!*

Sometimes I think Mr Cool must get a bit fed up with my wild Mabey imagination, but at least it makes things interesting for him. He can't ever complain about being bored, and he always has something to talk about in the staffroom.

The MCAS fan club was waiting for me outside.

"What did he say?"

"Did you get into trouble?"

"What was your picture of? Cats, I bet."

"No, it wasn't. It was completely related to the school curriculum." I tried to remember what Adam had been reading about. "It was a portrait of Pythagoras, from a mathematical perspective," I said. And I went off and left them open-mouthed, just like Mallory in the picture.

It *was* Mallory, of course. Mr Cool and I both knew that.

Oops.

Chapter Fourteen

MUM WAS IN AN EXTRA-GOOD MOOD after school, because she had a job interview lined up. "And this is *exactly* the sort of job I want," she said. "Not one of those huge law firms where I'd feel a hundred years too old, and way out of my depth."

Poor Mum. I had a vision of her, spluttering and waving her spindly hundred-year-old arms around in an outdoor swimming pool. And the lifeguard (who looked a bit like Karl Ballentyne) wasn't even looking; he was too busy watching Jessica, who was sunbathing in a very small bikini, while Zoe Watson was half drowning in the toddlers' pool.

When I tuned back in, Mum was saying, "It's a small two-person firm where they do a bit of everything. They've only just started up, but they're already looking to expand, so they want to take on a new graduate. And I didn't even have to answer an advertisement! They just rang up and asked if I'd like to apply." She was so excited, she couldn't stop talking. "The interview is tomorrow at ten o'clock. I hope I don't mess it up."

"You won't, Mum," I assured her. "You'll wow them. They'll be deeply impressed, and they'll probably offer you the job on the spot."

Afterwards, I realised I must have missed a bit, while I was thinking about lifeguards and swimming pools. I must have missed the crucial bit, about the name of the firm.

That night it was my turn to feed the cats. The air was full of soft thuds as they jumped down from their favourite spots all around the house and started heading for the kitchen. They were all very polite. There were no hisses, no scratching, no pushing or shoving. Uncle Theo had trained them well.

Just as I finished dishing out the cat food, a battery of knocks sounded at the front door. Ellie was standing there, beaming. "Did you mind me knocking like that? Adam said you would. He said it was rude."

"No, it was fine," I said. "It doesn't matter."

"See?" Ellie sent a triumphant look at Adam, who was deep in his book and didn't notice. It looked different from the one he'd been reading before. Adam was probably the sort of reader who got through several books a day, all of them five hundred pages long. "Did you have a good day at school?"

"It was okay."

"Mine wasn't," Ellie said cheerfully. "Mine was the most boring day in my whole entire life."

"Since Friday," Adam said. He marked his place with his finger and looked up. "Your mum said you've got cats. Ellie wants to meet them. If that's okay."

"Sure." I led them into the kitchen, where the cats were still eating.

"Is he deaf?" Adam asked, pointing at Oscar.

"I don't know. Why, should he be?"

"White cats with blue eyes usually are."

"Really? I never knew that."

"Often they have one blue and one orange eye, and then they're deaf on the blue side."

"How do you know?" I asked, but he just shrugged.

"Adam knows everything," Ellie explained. "He's full of fascinating facts."

Cleo leapt smoothly onto the chair beside us and started to clean herself. She was a beautiful cat: creamy-white all over except for her dark brown tail, paws, ears and face and clear blue eyes.

"Uncle Theo says her bowl has to be spotless, or she won't eat."

"She must be fussy," Ellie said. "She must be the fussiest cat in the whole world."

"Just fastidious," Adam corrected.

"Whatever that means," Ellie said. "You're just showing off, because you're reading the dictionary."

"*Are* you reading the dictionary?" I asked.

"Not right now," Adam said.

"He reads a page every night," Ellie said. "And he reads camera manuals. He's going to be a famous film director, like Peter Jackson, only even more famous. He's going to make lots of amazing films, and I'm going to star in all of them, aren't I, Adam?"

Adam didn't say *don't be ridiculous,* or *I'm not really that good.* He didn't look embarrassed. He just nodded and said, "That's right. As the gorilla."

"He's making a film right now, for a competition, and he's going to win it."

"Counting chickens." I was getting used to Adam's short sentences, and I figured he meant *Don't count your chickens until they're hatched.*

"It's not about chickens," Ellie said.

"So what is it about?" I asked.

Adam checked his page number. "It's a spoof – a take-off of a particular genre," he explained. "Like, a celebrity survivor show, but you film your family surviving without takeaways."

"You're not doing that one, are you?" Ellie asked anxiously.

"Or a love story, but with an ugly hero," Adam said. "Or a fairy tale where the wolf outsmarts Little Red Riding Hood."

"You should do that one," Ellie said. "I'd like to be Little Red Riding Hood."

"But you'd get eaten," Adam pointed out. "I'm doing a thriller. It's a take-off on a serial killer story, from the perspective of a family of birds, and the serial killer is a cat."

While Ellie stroked the cats, being very fair and giving them an equal number of pats each, Adam spouted more random facts, like *Sir Isaac Newton invented the cat door,* or *Cats sleep for approximately eighteen out of every twenty-four hours.*

"Siamese cats were first called Royal Cats of Siam, which was the old name for Thailand," he said. "According to legend, when the Royal Princesses of Siam went swimming in the river, they took off their rings and used their cats' tails as ring holders. That's why Siamese cats have a kink in their tail, to stop the rings from falling off."

"Maybe that's why Cleo is so fastidious," I said. "She thinks she's a Royal Princess."

A boy about my age, and a girl who was younger – it hadn't sounded very promising, but they might be an improvement on the Screechers after all. Ellie was bubbly and fun. Adam was pretty serious, but when he did smile, it was friendly and open; there was no slyness or trickery in it. Not like Mallory. If Mallory smiled at anyone, you always wondered *what does she want now?*

Dad came in as the two of them were leaving. "Who's this? Are you the local neighbourhood troops?"

"Yes, we are," Ellie answered for both of them again. "He's Adam and I'm Ellie."

"You can't read in that light," said Mum, which was what she always said, unless you were standing under a floodlight. If she wasn't going to study psychology, she could have retrained as an optometrist, but it was too late now. She was sitting in the lounge, peering out from behind teetering piles of boring textbooks, when she could have been surrounded by displays of the latest styles in glasses.

"It's light outside," Adam said, looking up briefly. "The moon rises at 5.37 tonight."

"You can just ask him, if you ever need to know anything," Ellie informed Dad.

"I'll remember that," Dad said.

But once they'd gone and he sat down with the paper his good mood evaporated. Every time a cat appeared he would tense up, worried that it was about to jump on him.

"Don't worry, Dad," I said. "They're all *nice* cats."

"Huh! There's no such thing," Dad said. "Don't forget, they're predators at heart. And they're out to get *me*."

Chapter Fifteen

MUM WAS EVEN MORE CHEERFUL AFTER HER job interview. "I think I did all right," she said. "They both seemed to like me."

"Of course they liked you," I said. "Why wouldn't they?"

"They were saying 'This will be your office,' as if they'd already decided."

"How many other people applied?" Dad asked.

Mum didn't know, but they didn't waste much time making their minds up. She came off the phone the very next afternoon bubbling over with excitement, not that you could see any bubbles, unless they were speech ones, tumbling out of her mouth.

"They've offered me the job! They want me to start next week!"

"Yay!" I gave her a big hug to celebrate the fact that we weren't going to starve to death. Cats arrived from all directions to see what the noise was about, and Tilda shot into a cupboard and hid behind a saucepan, peering out with startled eyes.

"Well done, darling!" Dad gave her a hug as well, and a big sloppy kiss. "Who are they, again?"

"The firm's called Page" – and then Mum made a noise like a machine breaking down – "Woz-Ziz-Click-Jetski and Associate."

"What?" I thought I hadn't heard right. I hoped I hadn't heard right. "Page and *who?*"

Mum repeated it. I had heard right.

"I told you the other day, didn't I? That's how they often name law firms. With the names of the partners, and the associate" – she looked a bit pink – "that's me, I suppose. There isn't anyone else, anyway, apart from the receptionist. One of the partners is Mr Page and the other one is Mr Woz-blah-blah-ski. Do you see?"

Yes, I saw all right. I didn't see everything, not right away. But I saw that Mallory's father was a lawyer, with his own law firm. My all-time archenemy's father had just offered my mother a job.

Wonderful. My life just got better. Not.

Next morning I walked into our classroom totally on edge, waiting for Mallory to make some smart comment about how my mum was going to be working for her dad. Mallory would just love that.

But she didn't say anything.

Maybe she was waiting for more people to turn up, so she could have a bigger audience for her smart comments. But when the bell went, she still hadn't said anything. She just ignored me, as usual, which today felt like quite a good option.

After a while, I figured Mallory might not even know. Probably her dad had no idea that I even existed, let alone that I was in his daughter's class. I hoped it wasn't like Mum's job in the restaurant, where they sat around and gossiped about their private lives. If I was lucky, Mallory might never find out that her dad was my mum's boss.

"Listen up, everyone," Mr Cool said, bouncing into the room all full of energy as though he'd already run a half-marathon before school.

Maybe he had. "Two important announcements." In our class, *important* usually equates to *sports-related*, so I prepared to tune out. "Nothing to do with sport," said Mr Cool, and everyone except me and Zoe groaned with disappointment.

"One . . ." Mr Cool ticked them off on his fingers, for people who had trouble counting. "Workplace Interview Day. Don't forget you have to bring me a proposal of who you intend to interview, preferably your parents at their place of work, or if not, a relative, friend or neighbour. You can do the interview at their home or even over the phone if you can't get to their work, but get it okayed by me first."

I stared at him in absolute disbelief. I'm hoping Mallory won't find out that her dad is my mum's boss, and Mr Cool is about to send her there to carry out a Workplace Interview. So much for being lucky; I should have known better. My last piece of luck was being chosen for the Charities Team with Jessica. Since then, my luck has run out completely.

And who will I interview? No way am I going to hang out at Page Woz-Woteva & Associate – but if I don't go there, who do I ask? Dad doesn't *have* a place of work, and Uncle Theo is out of the country.

Of course, Mr Cool might have forgotten that, and the absent-minded professors might not even notice if I went and sat in his office for an afternoon. That could be fun. I might absorb some philosophy at the same time and come away a deeper, more thoughtful person.

While I was trying to think deep, philosophical thoughts, I couldn't help noticing that half the class was zeroing in on Karl Ballentyne. Karl was smirking away, enjoying all the attention. His father's trendy restaurant in town was definitely the best place to do a Workplace Interview, because it could be carried out over pasta and pizza at lunch.

"Hey, Karl," voices were whispering, "have you got a partner?"

"Karl, can I come and interview one of your dad's cooks?"

"Me, me, Karl! Please, pick me!"

"And two ..." Mr Cool continued. It couldn't get any worse, could it?

It did get worse.

"Our visit to the TV studio workshop. You've all got the list of possible jobs, and I hope you're working on your CVs and job applications. This is just to let you know that for the newsreaders, we'll be choosing a boy-girl team."

There was a chorus of dismay, from the girls who'd been hoping to apply together, and from the boys who didn't want to be newsreaders because they had correctly deduced from the job title that they would need to be able to read.

"That's not fair, Mr Cameron. That's reverse sexism!"

"What? What? What have I missed?" cried Claudine, rushing in late. Aleesha leaned over to fill her in. "What? That's *totally* not fair!"

The howls of dismay gradually faded away into a horrified silence as the truth sank in: some girl was going to have to read the news with some boy. The status of newsreader was suddenly plummeting.

"Maybe I could be a camera operator," Jessica murmured. Jessica, behind a camera instead of in front of one? I don't think so.

Everyone looked round the room, visualising possible combinations. Callum and Aleesha? Matt and Claudine? Me and—?

School was just too complicated sometimes. Maybe I could tell Mum I wanted to be home-schooled. Instead of being trapped in a classroom drawing graphs or trying to play the ukelele, I could be making important scientific discoveries on my own.

The problem with that was I wasn't any good at Science.

The other problem was that kids who were home-schooled were often a bit odd and very clever. Like Adam. He was really nice, but you couldn't deny he was slightly unusual, and I got the impression that he was very, very smart.

I didn't want to be odd, and I wasn't that clever. It looked like I was stuck where I was.

Chapter Sixteen

IF MALLORY DID KNOW ABOUT MUM'S NEW job, she was saving it up for later, because everything else was overshadowed by the News of the Day. Mallory's crowd exchanged significant looks all morning, and talked in whispers just loud enough to make everyone else wonder what they were whispering about.

At lunchtime, it all came out: Piper was leaving. Her dad had got a new job and they were moving to another city; it was all happening very quickly. There were tears and group hugs (which I didn't join in) and promises to keep in touch, as though she was going to vanish in a puff of smoke that very second.

"I can't believe I won't be seeing you guys again," Piper said. "You've been the best friends ever."

"I can't believe you're going!" Claudine said. "Who will I hang out with at the pool?"

"Who's going to help us win our indoor netball?" Mallory said.

"We'll email you," Aleesha promised, "and we can look at your Facebook page and Skype you and everything."

"And you *will* see us again," Jessica said. "You can come back and stay in the holidays and we'll go shopping and stuff."

"You'll soon make new friends. I did," Mallory said.

"That's all lies – about her dad having a new job," I overheard Jessica whispering to Aleesha, when Piper went off to the office to pick up her school records. "My mum said he got made redundant and they had to sell their house. That's why they're moving, so they can go and live with her grandparents."

"Piper probably made them move, because she'd have nobody to do her Workplace Interview on," Aleesha whispered back.

The day she left, there were more group hugs and enough tears to flood the playground. "Bye!

Bye! I'll miss you!" Piper yelled out the window of her dad's car as she was driven away, and everyone yelled, "We'll miss you, too!"

It was funny, though. After all the drama of her departure, it didn't take long for her name to drop out of conversation. The Hawaiian Hula Hulas kept winning without her. Once or twice someone said, "Wonder what Piper's doing now?" but then they started talking about something else, like a new pair of earrings or what their annoying kid brother had done.

I hadn't joined in the group hugs when Piper left, and I didn't cry or scream when she drove away. But I thought about her a lot. I kept thinking about her being new somewhere else.

We'd never moved house, and I'd never moved schools. By now I knew every corner of every classroom, and every square centimetre of our grounds. I'd graduated from the little kids' sandpit and climbing frames to the adventure playground. I'd been at the adventure playground the day it was first opened, the same day that Callum fell off and had to go to hospital to have his head stitched up. I knew the best places to play hide and seek; I'd been into the staffroom; I'd been on duty in the first aid room; I'd done road patrol and been in all the school productions. Sometimes it felt boring, but it also felt sort of safe. Imagine not knowing *any* of that.

I wondered how Piper was getting on. I wondered if the girls at her new school loved having new girls.

On the weekend, Mum went looking for new work clothes while Dad and I did the weekly supermarket trip. We also had to visit the pet shop in town for Cleo's cat food, because she was too fussy (or fastidious) to eat the ordinary stuff.

The two of us are rapid and efficient shoppers because we both hate shopping. We had everything crossed off our list in record time and were heading back to the car when I bumped into them – literally. "Oof! Watch out," someone said, and it was Mallory.

Mallory and Jessica.

"What are *you* doing here?" Jessica said, as though there was some law that said I wasn't allowed within a hundred metres of a shopping centre.

I looked at all the plastic bags she was holding. "Well, I'm not wasting my money on useless consumer goods. I'm buying cat supplies."

"*What* supplies?" Mallory said.

"*You* know," Jessica said. "For all those cats she got from her crazy uncle."

Last year, Jessica could have said that and made it sound like a joke. But now it didn't sound like a joke any more.

"He's not crazy," I said, "and he's not using up the world's resources in plastic shopping bags, either." Mallory opened her mouth – no doubt to say something crushing – but I didn't wait to be crushed.

"Gotta go," I said, and I was out of there before she could turn to Jessica with raised eyebrows and a *what-next*? expression. More precisely, *what-will-that-crazy-Harriet-McDonald-do-next*?

So what? I didn't care. I got into the car and slammed the door.

"What was all that about?" Dad asked.

"No idea," I said, trying to look as innocent as possible.

"No idea? Why do I find those two words hard to associate with you?"

I shrugged.

"You don't go over to Jessica's much these days," Dad said. I thought he hadn't seen her, but he obviously had. "You used to love going round to see those animals of hers."

More silence. This time, I didn't even bother to shrug.

Mum's new job loomed over us all weekend. On Monday she left early to catch the bus, looking very smart (if not stick-thin) and nervous, but trying not to show it. On Monday night she came home excited but tired. Every day after that, she came home a bit more tired, and a bit less excited.

"What do you do there?" I asked. "Have you been to court? Do you stand up in front of the judge and win cases?"

But Mum said she didn't do any court work yet. She said she did a lot of paperwork, photocopying stuff and opening mail and filing documents. It sounded pretty boring to me, but Mum said you couldn't expect to start at the top. She said there was a lot of paper in a law office. In fact, she said, a law office *was* mostly paper.

"That sounds cool. Can I come and see it?" Imagine ... desks and chairs and computers and telephones and walls, all made of paper. Everything would be very white and clean, but easily damaged, and you'd get paper cuts in awkward places when you sat down.

"Soon," Mum said. "Not yet."

"What's Mr Woz-his-name like?"

"He's very nice," Mum said, but I didn't believe that. He was Mallory's father. He couldn't be nice at all. He was probably crooked, too; slippery and sneaky and totally untrustworthy. Just like Mallory.

Chapter Seventeen

THE GAP THAT PIPER HAD LEFT IN MALLORY'S gang (and the indoor netball team) closed up very quickly. Unfortunately, she'd also left a gap in the Leadership Teams.

Apart from Charities, which everyone knew was the best, there were lots of other teams: Magazine (second best), and Sports, and Cultural, and Library and Displays. They all had their good points – apart from Recycling, which everyone knew was the worst. Recycling was just a fancy name for Picking Up Litter. We called it the Rubbish Team, when Mr Bennett wasn't listening, and nobody wanted to be in it.

Because Piper had left, and a few other

people had come and gone in other classes, and probably because Mr Bennett had messed up to start with, the teams were now a bit unbalanced. In terms of membership, not mental content – although possibly that, too.

"So, what we're left with is a big gap in the Recycling Team," said Mr Cool. "Any volunteers? Hands up."

There was a sudden rush as everyone shoved their hands under their desks or anywhere else out of sight to make sure they didn't show at all.

"Hmm," said Mr Cool, looking around while everyone tried to avoid looking back. "Looks like I may have to make a unilateral decision."

"A what?" Callum whispered to Karl.

"Callum, right. Looks like you want to help save the planet. First volunteer."

"No!" Callum protested. "I don't care about saving the planet, do I?" He looked round for someone to back him up, but no one dared say anything.

Callum slumped back into his seat. "Great. Thanks for your support, everyone."

Mr Cool consulted his lists. "I may have to do a bit of juggling," he murmured to himself, and everyone winced.

"I can't do Recycling, it brings on my asthma," Georgia announced.

"Me neither, I get allergies," said Claudine, who doesn't.

Mr Cool ignored them. "What I'm thinking is ..." he said slowly, and we all held our breaths while we waited to hear. "I'm thinking that ... Mallory, we didn't get around to putting you in a team when you first arrived, did we?"

Mallory shook her head, and everyone else relaxed slightly. Mallory didn't look too concerned. She probably didn't know what a rubbish team it was.

"So we could put you in there, but we need at least one more ... and there are still a few too many people in the Charities Team." I saw Jessica stiffen. Mr Cool looked at his lists again. "Let's see, Jessica or Harry. One of you to join Callum and Mallory."

"Yeah, join them in the recycling bin," I heard Karl snigger.

Jessica chewed her lip. I'd known her for so long that I knew exactly what was going on in her mind. She was thinking: *want to be with Mallory ... want to stay in the cool and exciting Charities Team ... don't want to be in the lousy Recycling Team ... but want to do what Mallory's doing* .... She looked sideways at me, hoping I'd make the decision, but I wasn't going to help her out.

"Harry? Jessica? Which is it to be?" said Mr Cool impatiently, as if he couldn't wait to get onto the next thrilling event in the day's timetable.

Jessica still wasn't saying anything. Mr Cool looked at me and wiggled his eyebrows. "Harry?"

"Why not?" I said, shrugging. After all, the rest of my life was a disaster area. Being part of Recycling couldn't make matters much worse than they already were.

"Good. Thank you. I think we should have a Leadership Teams meeting soon," Mr Cool decided. "It's about time you all got together to set some priorities and organise a few activities."

"Cool!" Jessica said, relieved that she hadn't had to make a decision. She gave Mallory a *sorry-about-that* smile and leaned across to Renee and Latisha, her fellow Charities buddies.

"Hey, what about having a Bad Hair Day?" I heard Renee say.

"Or we could have a *Good* Hair Day, you know – straightest hair, longest plaits, smartest hair styles," Latisha suggested.

"Yeah, cool!" Jessica enthused, and they went into an intense huddle of planning cool activities that didn't involve rubbish.

"Great," Callum said. "I'll just go and climb into the recycling bin right now, shall I?"

Which was worse, being relegated to the Recycling Team? Or being in the same team as Mallory? It was hard to decide.

Chapter Eighteen

DAD STILL DIDN'T HAVE A JOB. HE SPENT A lot of time out in the garage tinkering with the car. It wasn't running very well, but Dad didn't mind too much because it gave him something to do when there wasn't any cricket on TV. Mum told him he should try retraining, like she had.

"Why don't you look for something different?" she suggested, but Dad wouldn't listen.

"I'm a builder, that's what I do," he said. "You can't teach an old dog new tricks."

Mum was preoccupied with her new job and Dad's animal phobia had got worse (if that were possible) so I was pretty much in charge of the cats. As soon as I got home from school, they would curl around my legs and fill the air with their rumbling purrs. Alfie or Lucy would often be sitting on the fence waiting for me, but none of them ever strayed very far, and they never got into fights with any other neighbourhood cats.

Every day I'd feed them, change their water and tidy up any messes, although there weren't many. Then I'd sit under a tree in the back garden and brush them, each in turn. That was my favourite part of the day. Whichever cat was on my lap would go into a sort of trance, giving out contented purrs that vibrated all the way down to my toes and up to my ears. Alfie, the one who liked kneading the computer keys at night, was a glossy black cat with a white bib. He was getting old and was a bit lazy and fat, but he loved being brushed. Lucy was a pretty tortoiseshell (tortoiseshells are always female, according to Adam), and she loved having the back of her head scratched.

From our garden, I could see over the hedge into next door. Sometimes I'd see Adam prowling around with his camera. He would lie down on his back on the ground, pointing it up at a tree; then climb the tree and aim the camera at one of the cats. If Ellie wasn't needed to help look after the twins, she often came across to give me an update on how annoying they'd been that day, how Adam's film was going, and how many books he was reading at the same time.

For several weeks, she was busy making Adam a birthday present. She brought it over to our place so he wouldn't see her working on it. It was a notebook made up of stapled-together pieces of paper, each page carefully ruled into sections.

"It's so he can write down the titles of all the books he ever reads," she explained. "There's a separate column for title, author and comments."

"You should have a column for number of pages, too," I said. "Then he can add up how many pages he's read each week."

"Good idea!" Ellie said, picking up her ruler. "Do you think he'll like it?"

"It's cool. I bet he will."

"He'd better," Ellie said darkly. "It's taken me hours and *hours*. If he doesn't say it's the best present he ever got, I'm going to tear it all up again. *You* never have to spend hours on stupid birthday projects like this," she added. "You're so lucky, being an only child. You must be the luckiest person in the whole world."

"What about all the other only children?" I asked.

"You must be luckier, because you're an only

child, plus you have all these cats to look after," Ellie declared. "It's not fair how lucky you are."

I thought Ellie was much luckier than me. There was her mum, at home looking after twins and a baby, and still managing to get dinner cooked in time. Dad was a terrible cook, and I wasn't much better. I always looked forward to Mum coming home, and not just because she could whip up a gourmet meal in ten minutes.

Usually she came walking down the road from the bus stop, but one evening, a gleaming new car pulled up outside. Mum got out, then leaned down and said something through the window. A tall man got out the driver's door. He was smoking a cigarette, and he looked vaguely familiar.

If it had been a movie, this would have been when the creepy music started. You'd know straightaway that he was going to be the villain.

You'd be even more certain, when he finished his cigarette and tossed the stub into the gutter. Not only was he a smoker – he was a litterbug as well!

"Hello-o! Jack ... Harry? Who's home?"

They were inside before I could duck out of sight, and that was when I realised where I'd seen him before: in our classroom talking to

Mr Cool, the day Mallory arrived at school.

"Oof!" his voice said, as he tripped over Max in the hallway.

"Harry, this is Mr Wojciechowski." Mum said it perfectly, with all the right clicking and machine-breaking-down noises, but I suppose you have to be able to pronounce your boss's name properly. "He kindly offered to drop me home from work. Alex ..." (that's what it sounded like, but later I found out his name was spelt Aleksander) "this is my daughter, Harriet."

There was a hiss and a yowl as Cleo, who'd been sitting on one of the kitchen chairs, stuck her kinked tail up in the air and went racing out the back door. Max skulked behind my legs, and Tilda skittered away with her paws going in all directions at once.

But I didn't need their opinion to work out what sort of person he was. The instant he came in, I could tell that he was mean and nasty and horrible. Exactly the right sort of father for his mean and nasty daughter. *Serves you right,* I thought.

Mallory's father was tall and perfectly dressed: smart jacket and tie, perfectly ironed shirt, perfectly pressed trousers, polished black shoes. He looked fit and tanned, and his hair was cut and streaked in a trendy sort of style. But I could tell his good looks were just a front. His nose was sharp, and his chin was sharp, and his eyes were very black and very sharp. His clothes smelt of cigarette smoke. His nose and his chin and his eyes said: *evil, mean, nasty, horrible.*

"Ah, Harriet," he said, holding out his hand for me to shake. I hate it when adults do that. They pretend that they're being polite, but really they're making fun of you. "I think you're in my daughter's class, aren't you?" Mr Woz said, plastering a fake smile on his face. His teeth gleamed like a wolf's. "That's a coincidence, isn't it? Mallory often mentions you."

I bet she does, I thought. So much for hoping he'd never find out about me.

"Is that right?" Mum said. "Harry, you never told me." She sounded disappointed that Mr Woz knew and she didn't. That made me feel bad, which was yet another thing to blame on Mallory.

Mr Woz looked around the room, with the fake smile still attached. His eyes gleamed too. "Have to like cats to live here, eh?"

Dad had come in from the garage without anyone noticing. "Can't stand them," he remarked, sticking out his hand. It was black with oil, and very grubby, and he didn't offer to wash it first.

Yay! I thought. At least Dad could see through him – and what an unpleasant thought that was, right up there with pig-hunting, flesh creeping and brains oozing out of heads sliced in half.

Mr Woz let out a short, sharp bark of a laugh, even though Dad wasn't joking. It sounded like the sort of noise a seal would make: one of those black, floppy, mean-looking ones. He stuck out a flipper, and after they'd shaken hands he held it up in the air, as though he didn't know where to put it without getting his clothes dirty.

Fortunately, Mr Woz didn't stay long, although it was long enough. He and Mum talked for a few minutes about some boring law stuff, and then he was climbing into his gleaming new car and driving away again. I went into the back garden to reassure the cats, who were prowling around looking agitated.

"Don't worry, Oscar," I said, stroking him. "It's all right, Alfie. You're quite safe here. He won't come back," I promised them.

I should have known I wouldn't be that lucky.

Chapter Nineteen

AFTER THAT, MR WOZ OFTEN DROPPED Mum home, and once or twice Mr Page did. Mr Page was short and plump, more like a penguin than a seal. Mr Woz made me feel as small as an insect, but Mr Page made me feel five years old. I half expected him to pat me on the head and produce a handful of sweets from his pocket, which he might have done if he could have remembered my name.

"Hello there," he would say greasily, "nice to see you ... Holly? Hayley?"

Mr Page was greasy and slimy and horrible. Mr Woz was mean and nasty and horrible, and he always left a lingering smell of smoke behind him. I wished Mum could have found another law firm to work in, but I couldn't say so when she was the one earning the money to feed us and pay the bills.

Dad and the cats kept out of their way. The cats retreated into the garden, and Dad went out to tinker with the car engine. I wondered if he was not fixing it on purpose, to give himself something to do. During the day he was working through a list of jobs Uncle Theo had left for him to do at his place – painting and fixing things – but he was starting to get a bit twitchy about not having a real job. Twitchy, the way that cats twitch the ends of their tails to show that they're feeling grumpy inside.

"They're nice people, Jack," Mum said. "Why don't you stay and talk to them?"

"Nothing to talk to them about," Dad muttered. "Not my sort of people."

I would have kept out of the way too, but I didn't want them snooping around without me. In all the legal shows on TV, the lawyers worked almost nonstop. They were there in the middle of the night, looking clever and exhausted but still immaculately dressed, searching for the vital piece of evidence that would win the case. That's what Mr Woz and Mr Page were meant to be doing, so why did they leave early and drop Mum home so often? That was what I wanted to know.

And wasn't it a bit strange, the way Mum had got the job? It wasn't advertised; they'd got in touch with *her*, and we never knew how many other people, if any, they'd interviewed. Something about it didn't feel right to me.

Nobody else seemed to suspect anything.

"Don't you think they come round here an awful lot?" I grumbled to Mum.

"No," Mum said. "They just drop me home now and then, that's all. It's very kind of them. They're just being friendly." She didn't seem to have noticed that he was mean and nasty and horrible.

"Now and then?" I said. "They're here all the time, snooping around. They're *too* friendly."

"Harry! They don't *snoop*," Mum said.

"Yes, they do. Snoop, snoop, snoop," I said.

Mum couldn't see anything wrong with Mr Woz. "He's a nice man, and an excellent boss," she always said. (She never mentioned the fact that she was being poisoned at work by second-hand smoke.)

But I was suspicious. That very day, there was a story in the newspaper (which I knew because we'd done it in News at school and it wasn't about sport so I paid attention for once) about a lawyer being sent to prison for swindling his clients out of all their retirement savings. Lawyers were always in the news, being arrested for embezzlement, or for striking dodgy deals with gang members.

What if Mr Woz and Mr Page ran that sort of firm? What if they employed Mum because they knew she was good at paperwork, but she was so honest and unsuspecting that they'd still be able to pull the wool over her eyes? My imagination got a bit confused at that point, mixing up paper and wool.

But it was a month or so later when my imagination really went to work.

Dad wanted to pick up some stuff at the big hardware store across town, and I went along to keep him company. We came back using the shortcut through the airport. You have to slow down to drive past the entrance and, just as we did that, a taxi pulled up. The taxi driver jumped out and went round to the boot. A vaguely familiar figure climbed out of the passenger seat and stood there, smoking, while he waited for the driver to finish unloading the luggage. A tall, lean figure, perfectly dressed, fit and tanned. Streaked fair hair. Sharp nose, sharp chin, sharp eyes.

I looked quickly at Dad, but he was watching the cars in front and hadn't noticed. We were right alongside the taxi now. I slid down in my seat and wound down my window.

"That everything, sir?" the taxi driver asked. Mr Woz nodded briefly, dropped his cigarette stub (litterbug!) and handed over some money. The taxi driver stowed it away.

"Well, have a good trip, sir. Thailand, isn't it? That'll be nice, this time of year."

Good! I thought. *He's going to Thailand. That means he won't be able to snoop round our place for a while.*

Then I thought: *Thailand? Why is he going there? For a holiday? So why is he going without Mallory? For business? Mum hasn't said anything about them doing business in Thailand.*

Mr Woz gave a brief nod and turned away. He lifted a hand in a wave, and I saw another figure – short, plump, penguin-like – climbing out of a second taxi.

My imagination was working overtime at this point, and that's not necessarily a good thing. No work (as in Dad's case) is bad, but too much work can be bad as well. My overworked imagination was asking: *Why are they both going to Thailand? What do people go to Thailand for?*

Temples ... elephants ... beaches ... and ... *drugs?*

Now I started getting *really* suspicious. Putting two and two together. Most people at that point get four, which is theoretically correct, but those of us with wild imaginations sometimes get five. And what's wrong with that? That's how all great discoveries are made. Christopher Columbus wouldn't have discovered America without a wild imagination to spur him on; he'd have stayed home like everyone else. Sir Isaac Newton would have eaten the apple that fell on his head, Einstein would have given up on relativity and the Wright Brothers wouldn't have believed they could fly.

Somewhere between airport and home, the ideas that were niggling in my head came into focus. I lined them all up, fitted them together and made a gigantic leap of the imagination – which means that imagination maybe isn't like a lion, or a cheetah, or a dog, or a kite, or any of those things. It's more like a gazelle or an antelope that can leap vast distances. People talk about having a powerful imagination, and power is something that people admire in swimming or rugby, so why not when it comes to imagination?

When I put two and two together in a *different* way, everything started to point to Mr Woz and Mr Page. They were rich. They were lawyers. They were mean, horrible and nasty, and bound to be involved in something illegal. And they were going to Thailand.

Not to mention the fact that Mr Woz smoked, and everyone knows smokers are unpleasant and selfish, because they ruin the environment for everyone else. As a member of the Recycling Team, I took that very seriously.

In a flash, I had it. They were sure to be drug runners. Or drug smugglers, or both (I wasn't sure what the difference was, if there was a difference).

That might seem quite a big leap but if it does, you probably don't have much of an imagination. To me it was clear as the answer to a simple maths problem. Mean Mallory's Dad + Smoker + Going to Thailand + Crooked Lawyers in the News = only one answer.

They were definitely crooked – and probably big-time drug dealers as well. My mother was working for a firm of crooked, drug-running lawyers.

Chapter Twenty

THIS WAS SUCH A SCARY THOUGHT – MY mother, innocently trapped in a corrupt, drug-dealing law practice – that I tried hard to push it to the back of my mind. That makes my mind sound like a wardrobe with everything neatly tidied away, but it's probably more like the mess on my bedroom floor. I shoved the scary thought under a pile of dirty washing, and tried to ignore it.

At least Mr Woz and Mr Page were out of the way, so they wouldn't be snooping around for a while, and Dad wouldn't have to keep hiding out in the garage. Mum was happy (but tired) because she had a job, although she hadn't yet cottoned onto the true nature of her employers, and the job wasn't quite as exciting as she had hoped. Meanwhile, school was as depressing as ever, or possibly more depressing, since my transfer into Recycling.

"Where's Mallory's dad?" I asked Mum, pretending Mallory had told me he'd gone away. I didn't let on that we'd seen him at the airport, or that I knew where he'd gone.

"He's away somewhere on business, or a conference or something," Mum said vaguely.

Didn't she know where he'd gone? "Are you in charge, then?" Oops. That showed I knew Mr Page had gone as well. But Mum didn't notice.

"Yes, but there's not much happening right now. It's a quiet time of year."

Suspicious – they hired Mum, even though they knew there wasn't enough work for her. What a waste of all that hard work she'd put into her law degree. They probably thought she was too naive to catch on to their underhand, illegal work.

I decided to tackle Mallory about it. Not a real tackle, although it was an attractive thought. "I see your dad's gone away," I said.

Mallory shrugged. A sort of *so-what, don't-*

bother-me shrug. "He goes away all the time." (Sub-text: *my father travels a lot because he is a highly qualified and very important lawyer, and your father does – what, exactly?*)

"So where's he gone this time?"

Mallory shrugged again. "Dunno, somewhere."

I know where, but you don't. Hasn't he told you? Highly suspicious.

Mr Woz obviously didn't want to involve Mallory in his illegal drug-dealing activities. That showed some fatherly concern, but it wouldn't help much when he was sent to prison.

I didn't know much about Mallory's family, seeing as she'd arrived too late to draw her Family Tree. Her mum never picked her up from school, or came on school trips, or turned up in the playground. If she wasn't around, Mallory would be too young to be left home alone. She'd have to be sent to some kind of institution (did they still have orphanages?) or a foster home. I wondered if that would make her a nicer person.

There were other things I didn't know about Mallory, such as:

1. Where does she live?
2. When's her birthday?

3. Does she have any pets?

4. Do I care?

And the answers would be don't know, don't know, don't know and no.

I wasn't going to ask, either. That would make it seem as though I was interested, and I wasn't. Not a bit.

Until now, I had been successfully putting off our Conservation topic, but I couldn't put it off much longer, because we were due to present it in another few days. I'd come across another really good idea – or better than my Loch Ness monster idea, anyway – wildlife smuggling of birds and birds' eggs.

There was a programme about it on TV, and I'd gone onto the Internet to find out more. **Growth in illegal bird smuggling**, the headlines read. **Illegal bird trade. Trade in smuggled wildlife increases. Parrot Police on the alert.**

Apparently, wildlife smuggling is worth billions of dollars a year, but lots of smuggled birds and animals die from bad handling or stress or suffocation. It's hard to smuggle live birds, so people smuggle the eggs instead. Then they raise the birds when the eggs hatch, and export them legally. A breeding pair of birds can be worth tens of thousands of dollars.

I told Mallory all this, but she had her own ideas. She wanted to do the endangered giant snail. "Some people were protesting about it on the news," she said. "There's this new opencast coal mine that's going to threaten its habitat and maybe cause its extinction. A snail is *way* more important than a coal mine."

It was *so* annoying. I felt like saying 'That's my idea!' but there was no way she would believe me, especially when I'd just been raving on about bird smuggling.

"We could cut out a snail-shaped piece of card, and make the writing go round and round inside the shell," Mallory said.

"Too hard to read," I growled.

"But it would *look* good."

A few minutes later, Mr Cool walked past. "Decided what you're doing?" he asked.

"*I* want to do the endangered giant snail," Mallory said.

Mr Cool raised one eyebrow. "Interesting idea," he remarked, looking at me. I didn't say anything.

We worked on, side by side: Mallory on her snails, me on my smuggled birds' eggs, in a tense silence. I was fuming inside, and it didn't help that another thought kept knocking at the edges of my cross mood, like one egg nudging up against another egg in a saucepan of boiling water. *You ought to give in,* this thought said.

I was *not* going to give in. I still liked the idea of the endangered giant snail, slithering slowly on in the face of opencast coal mining, but I wasn't going to tell Mallory so, because it was *my* idea to start with. And now I'd had a *better* idea.

On the other hand – if Mallory suddenly said *she* would give in, how was I going to feel then? Mean and Nasty and about as small as a worm.

It was Mallory who was Mean and Nasty, not me.

The two eggs that were rattling in the saucepan of my imagination nudged each other so sharply that one of them cracked and all this white stringy stuff spilt out. Disgusting. I threw down the felt pens, folded my arms crossly and turned to Mallory.

"All right! We can do your stupid snails!" I snarled, just as she turned to me and said, "All right! We'll do your stupid birds' eggs!"

"So, what's the big decision?" Karl asked, leaning over to see what we were doing.

Mallory tore up her sheet of paper. "Birds' eggs," she snapped.

"Snails," I said, turning my drawing over and starting to sketch out a snail shell instead.

"*We've* got a great topic, eh, Karl?" Callum said. "We're doing—" but Karl stuck his big hand over Callum's big mouth before he could tell. I was so busy watching Karl dragging Callum away that I didn't notice Mallory reaching over to grab my snail shell sketch until she screwed it up and tossed it away. The ball of paper floated through the air, over four desks and landed neatly in the rubbish bin.

The two of us glared at each other.

"What was that for? We're doing your snails," I said.

"We're not," Mallory said, through gritted teeth.

I gritted mine as well. "Yes. We. Are."

Chapter Twenty-one

AFTER A TENSE FEW DAYS OF ENFORCED cooperation, we started presenting our topic animals. Tina told us about tigers. Jessica contributed a few sentences, printed straight off Wikipedia. Other kids did rhinoceroses, gorillas and elephants. We had animals being killed for their coats, or ground up for use in traditional medicines. It was all a bit depressing, and made you think there would soon be no animals left at all.

Then it was our turn. I unfolded my notes and stood up. "We're going to talk about some of our native flora and fauna. In particular, the endangered giant snail."

Flora and fauna was such a nice phrase. *Flora* sounded like a little Victorian girl, and *fauna* like something out of the Narnia books. I'd wanted to say it at least once, but after that I was going to stick to *plants and animals,* in case nobody understood what it meant.

"Aren't you going to talk about the endangered domestic cat?" Karl asked. He and Callum nudged each other and snickered, like they had some secret joke going on. I didn't pay any attention, which wasn't hard because Karl has been annoying me since kindergarten and I've learnt to ignore him.

"*Powelliphanta* land snails . . ."

"What? Elephant snails?" Matt interrupted.

". . . are called living fossils because they've been around for like 200 million years. They are carnivorous, slurping up slugs and worms, and some of them are huge – ten centimetres across – which is as big as a hamburger."

"Eww," said Claudine.

Some of the girls shrieked. The boys licked their lips and patted their stomachs.

"Snailburgers, yum."

"Gross," said Aleesha.

Mallory's turn: "A whole lot of these snails had to be moved because the area where they lived on Mt Augustus was in the way of a coal mine."

"Why didn't they just squash them?" said Karl. *Why doesn't someone just squash you?*

My turn again, and for once I hadn't lost my notes. The whole class was hanging on my every word. As I talked, I imagined the words floating out of my mouth like big balloons, and everyone in the class grabbing a string and hanging onto it. Soon the classroom would be full of word balloons, bobbling up against the ceiling. Nobody had listened to me so intently all year.

"They had to capture thousands of snails and eggs" – this was a bit hard to read, because my writing went round and round the snail shell – "and look after them while they dug up the dirt where they used to live and moved it about eight hundred metres north, where they released them back into their new home."

Which must have been a bit weird for the snails. Living up on Mt Augustus for hundreds of generations, suddenly taken away and then put back somewhere that was their new home and their old home at the same time.

Mallory again: "They tagged some of the released snails with miniature radio transponders and antennae, so they could keep track of them. The only problem was that the transponders are glued to their shells, which might interfere with mating when one snail climbs on top of—"

There was a lot of screaming and laughter. Mallory rolled her eyes and waited for the noise to die down. I was actually starting to sympathise with Mr Cool at this point. It was very hard to keep everyone on track. Mr Cool was trying, not very hard, to hide a smug smile, as though pleased that I was realising this at last.

"Some people thought it cost too much money to move them, but other people thought they shouldn't have been moved at all." I finished quickly, folded up my notes and sat down again. Everyone was surprisingly quiet. All my word balloons went bobbling out the door and into the playground, and floated away into the sky. A flock of sparrows flew past, chirping, and popped some of them.

"Thank you, Harry and Mallory," Mr Cool said. (*Harry and Mallory*. The first time those two names had been mentioned in the same breath in our classroom, and probably the last.) "You've presented a very clear picture of the conflict between development and conservation, and given us all a lot to think about. Who's next? Karl."

Karl and Callum got up, grinning their heads off. "We're going to talk about endangered birds," Callum said.

Karl held up a **Wanted** poster with a picture of a tabby cat on it. The caption was written in Karl's terrible handwriting so it was hard to read.

Matt slowly spelled it out. "Did you ... know ... that your car ... could be a killer?" He looked confused."We're not doing Road Safety, are we?"

"Not your car, your *cat*," Karl said, waving the poster round in front of my face. They went on with great enjoyment to list some highly unreliable facts and figures about the number of native birds and animals killed by domestic cats.

"*That is so not true!*" I said. "Anyway, you're supposed to keep your cats *in* overnight. *Everyone* knows that."

"Let's take a quick survey," Karl said. "How many people here keep their cats inside overnight?"

One hand went up. Mine.

Chapter Twenty-two

THAT WAS THE SAME DAY I WAS THROWN out of Mallory's lunchtime gang. Or perhaps I threw myself out, like throwing yourself out of a plane for a skydive. I wasn't sure if I was still falling, screaming through the air, or if I'd already landed with a thump – but knowing my luck, I'd land in the middle of a cowpat, not a haystack.

"Pa's just bought us a new house," Mallory told everyone. "In Forest Road. It's huge, and it used to be owned by this crazy old guy. As crazy about birds as some people are about cats, you know?" Very funny, they all laughed; of course they knew. "It's got these enormous empty bird cages out the back—"

"Aviaries," I said.

They were all clustered around her: Jessica, Aleesha, Claudine, Tina and a few others. Tina looked puzzled, as though this was yet another strange word she'd never heard before. The others looked round with *huh?-did-someone-say-something?* expressions on their faces. Then they looked at Mallory, to check if they were supposed to pay any attention to me. Mallory rolled her eyes, as though she'd just been asked for her hundredth autograph, but these constant interruptions were the price of fame. She half turned her back on me and opened her mouth to continue.

Huh, yourself, I thought. *Don't just ignore me.* "They're not bird cages," I said. "The proper name for them is aviaries."

As soon as I said it, I realised it was a mistake. Mallory smiled, a sly, victorious smile, and went on: "It has five bedrooms and three bathrooms, and my bedroom has an ensuite. The proper name for that is *ensuite,*" she informed her fan club. "And it has a spa bath as well, the proper name for which is *spa bath.*"

Of course the fan club was rolling round in stitches by now. (All except for Tina, who still looked puzzled.) A teacher on lunchtime duty came past with a string of small children attached. "My, you girls are having a good time this afternoon, aren't you?" she said, before the littlies dragged her away. Mallory waited till she was out of earshot before continuing.

"And in the back garden – the proper name for that is *back garden* – next to all the bird cages – and the proper name for them is" – she made a mock bow in my direction, and enunciated very carefully – "*aviaries*" – at which the fan club howled even louder – "my Pa is going to put in a trampoline, the proper name for which is—"

"*Trampoline!*" they all chorused.

"Oh, ha ha," I muttered.

Well, that was it. I was sick of hanging about on the fringes of Mallory's fan club, hoping they'd come to their senses and see her for what she really was. I turned my back on them just like that, thinking: *I should have done this weeks ago*, and went off to find some other group to hang out with till the bell went.

Only it wasn't as easy as all that.

I couldn't hang out with the boys, that was obvious. All they ever did was charge around being non-stop loud and stupid. Anyway, they were boys.

I liked the little kids, but doing buddy class

with them once a week was enough. I wasn't going to hang out with them for the whole of lunchtime, and I didn't want to read in the library for a whole hour, either. Maybe I could be like Adam and walk round with a book. Except that when he did that, he just looked like Adam being Adam, whereas I would look like a total loser.

Eating a pot of yoghurt for an hour is boring, even if you like yoghurt, which I don't. Talking about TV, boys and/or Mr Cool would be even more boring. I didn't have anyone to text, and I wasn't going to shoot (and miss) goals all lunchtime, either.

I didn't feel like joining any of those other groups, even if they'd wanted me. But it's hard work, not being in a group without looking like a loser. You have to look purposeful all the time, as though you're on your way somewhere, or have been asked to do something for a teacher. The minute you start to mooch, you're done for. You might as well have a neon sign on your forehead saying *Warning. Do not Approach. Not in a Group. Groupless State May be Catching.*

I've often thought the groups should have to move around, like a dinner Mum and Dad went to once, where everyone got up and sat next to someone new after each course. That way, the boring groups wouldn't be quite so boring, and the fun groups would get to share the fun. The boys wouldn't monopolise the soccer ground. The TV addicts would realise there was more to life than TV (they might even read a book), and Mallory's fan club would realise there was more to life than trotting after her like sheep.

That's just one of my good ideas, and I'm full of them. I think I'd be just as good at running the school as the principal. Perhaps I could spend the rest of this lunch hour having a little chat to him. I'd go up to his office and he'd say, "Harriet McDonald, isn't it?"

"Harriet Jasmine Emerald Florence Mabey McDonald, actually, but just call me Harry," I'd tell him.

"Come in Harry, what can I do for you?"

"No," I'd say, "it's what I can do for *you*, Mr Principal," which is not his real name but I don't want to ruin his promotion prospects, because then he might get promoted somewhere else. "Just leave everything to me, it will all be fine," I'd say, "and you can go off and run some little lawn-mowing operation or dairy somewhere."

No, I couldn't do that because he'd be having lunch in the staffroom, not working in his office.

I still thought it was a good idea though. Maybe when we moved all the groups around, we could include the teachers, and we'd get to share in their yummy morning teas. They're always having treats for any old reason: birthdays or engagements or new babies. Mr Cool often comes back into class still finishing off a slice of banana cake or chocolate brownie (his second piece, I bet), and it always looks better than whatever we've just dug out of our lunchboxes.

Up till now, I'd hung around on the edges of Mallory's group, putting up with being ignored or laughed at for the sake of occasionally being allowed to join in. But now that I'd walked off and left them and there wasn't any other group to join, my only option seemed to be to find somewhere to hide every lunchtime from now on.

Or maybe I could get a special dispensation, like Claudine for her swimming. I could explain that Dad needed me for urgent cat-related duties, because of his deep psychological aversion to animals, and I could ask him to tear down the road with the horn blasting at precisely 12.30 pm every day and pick me up.

As if on cue, our car went rattling past with Dad looking stressed at the wheel. I waved but he didn't see me. As the bell finally went, after what must have been the longest lunch hour on record, there were more gales of laughter from Mallory's group.

"... people who are crazy about cats" – her voice carried clearly – "and the proper name for *them* is..." and she said something to the others, covering her mouth with her hand as she said it.

But she was looking straight across the playground, right at me.

Chapter Twenty-three

"I THINK," ELLIE SAID, "THAT THE PROPER name for her is b—"

"Ellie!" Adam said.

"What? It's not rude to state a fact."

"Opinion," Adam said, frowning at his book. "Anyway, you're not supposed to know words like that. So let's pretend you don't."

Dad was in the garage, cleaning the car, which obviously still worked in emergencies. He'd been taking Tilda to the vet for her vaccinations and she'd been sick all over the back seat. He wasn't happy. Adam, Ellie and the cats were helping me to recover from my traumatic lunchtime. Polly was purring deep, contented purrs on my lap;

Ellie was tossing the toy mouse for a completely recovered Tilda to play with; Adam was reading, with his back against a tree; and Cleo was watching us from up in the branches.

"The proper name for her is *witch*, then," Ellie said. "It rhymes. Anyway, she sounds totally evil. She sounds like the meanest, most evil person in the whole world."

"She is," I said. "Possibly in the whole universe."

"She thinks she's a Big Shot, but she's not," Ellie said. "Deep inside, she's the Smallest Shot that ever was. I bet she's secretly scared of Harry and her Magical Mabey Hair."

"It's not magical," I said. "This is the sort of hair they warn you about in shampoo advertisements."

"I bet she's as mean as a pinball machine." Ellie tied a piece of string to the tail of the toy mouse. She jumped up and ran round the courtyard, dragging it along for Tilda to chase. Tilda skittered after her. "Mean, mean, mean as a pinball machine," Ellie sang. "I can't wait to meet her."

"You won't," I said.

"Yes, I will," Ellie said, "on the Sports Exchange. When our school comes to play your school. Haven't you been told about that yet?"

"Maybe. If it was anything to do with sport, I probably wasn't listening."

Adam looked up from his book. "Mallory," he said briefly. "Sounds like mallow."

"Marshmallow?" Ellie fell back into the seat beside us, as Tilda skidded up against her ankles and pounced on the mouse.

"No, a herb, you ignorant sibling," Adam said.

"A bitter one, I hope," I said, feeling a lot better now I'd got the whole lunchtime saga off my chest (although you'd have to wonder why it should be on your chest, and not your shoulders, or your forehead, or some other place).

"That big old place, near the end of Forest Road," Adam added, "... been empty for ages." He always knew what we were discussing, even when he was engrossed in his book. Forest Road wasn't very far away, but it was a posh street and I didn't often go down there. Maybe Adam spent a lot of time exploring the local neighbourhood, when he'd finished his home schooling for the day.

"*That* place?" Ellie said. "It's huge!"

Mallory's voice echoed in my head. "It has five bedrooms and three bathrooms, with ensuites and a spa bath. And aviaries," I said.

"Aviaries ..." Adam said. "They would be a cool place to film in."

"Even better if they're empty," I said without thinking.

He looked at me. "Harry, you're a genius."

"Not another one," Ellie groaned, but Adam was fired with enthusiasm.

"So creepy ... those empty roosts would make a brilliant final sequence, totally apocalyptic."

"Apo-what?" Ellie said. "Can you try and remember that we're not all walking dictionaries?"

"Last things," Adam said. "Disasters. End of the world."

"Wouldn't it be trespassing?" I asked doubtfully, but Adam just shrugged.

"No one's living there."

"What are you reading about now?" I asked quickly, before he reverted to two-word sentences.

"The origins of the universe. And black holes."

Sometimes it felt as though Uncle Theo had fallen into a black hole. He was never very good at keeping in touch, but on this trip he was even worse than usual. There were no phone calls, no emails, no letters, no postcards. Maybe he was too engrossed in his fascinating philosophical discussions. "We've lost track of Theo lately," Mum had said the night before, and I thought, *another thing to add to the list*.

"I'll come with you," Ellie said. "I want to see where Mean Old Mallory is going to be living. Maybe I can cast a niceness spell on her bedroom."

"Doubt it," I said. "It would have to so strong it would bring the whole house down."

That was how we came to be sneaking around the back of Mallory's new house a few days later. I told Dad that we were going out, but he was busy talking to Ellie's dad about something and didn't pay much attention. He said "Okay, fine," when *No, stupid idea* would have been much better advice.

It was huge; the biggest house in a street of big houses, with a double garage out the front and a grand front entrance. The 'For sale' sign had SOLD plastered across it.

"Are you *sure* we're allowed to do this?" I said, but the others had already squeezed down the side by the hedge, and I didn't want to be left by myself. We found ourselves in the huge back garden, full of tall trees and even a fishpond, with the aviaries tucked away in the far corner of the lawn.

It was very quiet. A few sparrows hopped around on top of the aviaries, and one appeared to be trapped inside. "Wait!" said Adam, and he lifted his camera up close to the wire mesh. "Perfect," he murmured. "Okay, you can open the door now." The little sparrow flew out, chirping, and we walked in.

"Ew," Ellie exclaimed. "The ground's covered with droppings. And it *stinks*."

"It's a nice smell," I said. "A bird smell."

"Actually," Adam said solemnly, "the proper name for that is avian."

Ellie's giggle turned into a gasp when we heard doors slamming out on the street. The next thing we heard was the gate opening, and voices on the front path.

"Help!" Ellie squealed.

"Quick, we'd better hide," I said. I could imagine it getting round school tomorrow, courtesy of Mallory: Harry McDonald is so totally crazy, she's taken to hanging out in empty bird cages. Oh, sorry, the proper name for them is, of course, aviaries.

The three of us scrabbled for the door. It

wouldn't open. My heart was going *thump, thump, thump*. We were going to be trapped, just like the sparrow. But it shot open just in time, and we tore back across the lawn and crouched down behind the hedge.

"That's him, isn't it?" Adam whispered. "I've seen him dropping your mum off. Who's that fat guy? Is he the real estate agent?"

But it wasn't. It was Mr Page. We could see the two of them, one tall head and one shorter one, peering out the windows. Suddenly our expedition seemed like a really bad idea. I could imagine Mr Woz withering us with some sarcastic comment, while Mr Page shook his head as if we were naughty toddlers.

"What if they go upstairs?" Ellie half shrieked. "They'll see us from there."

"What if they don't?" Adam said, but I didn't feel that was much help.

"We could go back the way we came," Ellie said.

"The real estate agent might be out there, waiting," I said.

"Just as long as they don't come out *here*," Ellie said.

No such luck. There was the sound of keys fitting into a lock again, and the back door opened. We ducked further back into the shadow of the bushes.

"More bird poop," Ellie wailed.

"Shut up!" Adam elbowed her in the ribs, and she fell over.

"Ewww! Yuck!"

Mr Woz and Mr Page stood on the back deck, surveying the scene. Their voices travelled over the lawn to us.

"I see what you mean ... terrible smell ..."

"All have to come out ..."

"Unless ... been thinking ... *murmur murmur* ... might be able to ..." That was Mallory's dad. What did he mean? Might be able to *what*?

"Got pins and needles." Ellie was making funny faces. "Ah ... ah ... going to sneeze ..."

"Don't!" I whispered fiercely. Ellie gulped. Her eyes watered. A few seconds later, the sneeze burst out, but luckily they'd gone back inside.

We didn't move till we heard the front door open and shut, and the car drive off. We squeezed along by the hedge and peered out cautiously to make sure the coast was clear. None of us said a word until we were well down the road.

"Phew!" Ellie breathed. "That was the scariest time I've ever had in my whole life!"

Adam was lost in storyboarding his movie,

and now that I'd recovered from the fear of being caught in a very embarrassing situation, I was busy thinking. Looking at that huge house had made me even *more* suspicious. They'd just been to Thailand, and now Mr Woz had bought an expensive house with aviaries out the back, and he wanted to keep them, not knock them down, because they might be useful.

It was obvious, wasn't it? They weren't just drug smugglers. I bet they were also *wildlife* smugglers … and illegal importers of birds' eggs!

Chapter Twenty-four

"HARRY ..." MUM SAID, "YOU KNOW how Mallory's family has bought that big old place in Forest Road?"

Oops! They'd spotted us after all! They'd already rung Mum to complain, and she was going to be struck off because we'd been trespassing. (Being struck off is what happens to a lawyer if they do something wrong. It's not an actual blow, more a psychological one.) Mum would lose her new job, and I'd have two unemployed parents again.

"Ye-es," I said, carefully. "I think I heard Mallory talking about it."

"Alex was telling me how they're a bit worried

about their cat," Mum said. (Phew! They hadn't spotted us.) "It's a Siamese, like Cleo; quite highly strung, and they think it will get unnerved with all the renovations they're planning on doing. They're renting at the moment, and I thought it would be nice if we offered to look after the cat here, just until the building work is finished."

One part of my mind thought: *no, it would not be nice!* Our own house – the one place where I could count on getting away from evil Mallory Woz-Zip-Zapski, if not her father – was about to be invaded by the enemy.

Anther part thought: *soooo ... Mallory does have a cat – ah ha!* She'd kept that pretty quiet. Then again, Mallory had been the one person apart from Mr Bennett I hadn't bothered asking when I did my Pet Name Survey.

"Why here?" I said. "Cleo might not want another Siamese around. *Dad* might not want another Siamese around. There are plenty of catteries they could take it to."

"That's not very gracious, Harry. We *are* just around the corner – and they know us. It's very convenient for them."

It wasn't very convenient for me, but I got the feeling there wasn't much point objecting. Probably Mum had already made the offer.

"They're going to bring it round tonight," Mum said.

"Tonight?" I was right. "I bet it's got a stupid name."

Mum just looked at me. "What is it you have against Mallory, Harriet?"

"I was talking about their cat," I said. "I didn't mention Mallory, but seeing as you did, I've got nothing against her except a perfectly natural reaction based on her temperament, which is thoroughly evil and nasty."

"That's not the way I see her when she comes into the office," Mum said. "She seems a perfectly nice girl to me. I wish you'd try harder to be friends with her."

"She has plenty of friends," I said. "She doesn't need any more."

Mr Woz and Mallory both turned up with their highly-strung Siamese. They must have had some big fight before Mr Woz persuaded Mallory to come along. She got out and slammed the door of their smart, shiny car in a "why'd-you-make-*me*-come?" way.

Well, why *did* you come? I thought.

Dad had escaped. He'd gone to talk to Ellie's dad about something, but Adam was out filming in their front garden. He pointed the camera in Mallory's direction as she stalked up the path, and she glared at him.

Mum's back was turned, so she couldn't see Mallory rolling her eyes when she offered Mr Woz a coffee, or her *let's-get-out-of-here-as-soon-as-possible* expression. They started to talk about some case they had on at work. I was sidling out the door, about to make my escape so I could look at Mallory's filthy look captured on Adam's camera, when Mum said, "Harry! Why don't you and Mallory take Blue Streak out and let him get used to some of the other cats?"

"Blue Streak?" I said it very clearly and politely, but I knew Mallory would be able to translate my real meaning, which was *what a ridiculous name!*

"Pedigree name is longer, of course, but we call him that because he's a blue-pointed Siamese," Mr Woz said. "Heard the saying 'go like a blue streak'? Simply means go very fast, basically." Mr Woz obviously liked defining things. Perhaps it was a side effect of being a lawyer.

Blue Streak was mewing inside his travelling box on the floor.

"You carry him," I said to Mallory. Once again, I used a perfectly civil voice, so Mum and

Mr Woz didn't notice anything, but Mallory and I both knew it meant *one-up to me.*

I led the way into our back garden, which was much smaller than the enormous one at her new house. All the cats followed us, except for Cleo who was already there, looking down at us from a tree. Mallory put Blue Streak's cat box down without letting him out. She was looking round, about to say something cool and cutting, in her usual style.

I braced myself for it. Mallory turned round. Her eyes were glowing, and her voice sounded quite different.

"This is *so* cool. *Look* at all your cats," she said.

She sank down on a garden seat, still gazing round with those glowing eyes. Cleo climbed down from her tree, then quietly padded over and leapt gracefully up onto Mallory's knee. She turned round a few times, kneading herself a comfortable spot, and settled herself, staring at me with a smug expression on her face.

This was unbelievable. Cleo did not normally like strangers. It was so annoying that I couldn't tell if I was more annoyed at Mallory or at Cleo.

"Have you always had them all?"

"Yes. No. They belong to my uncle really, but he—" I was babbling, so I pulled myself together. Probably Mallory was just pretending. She wanted to find out so she could laugh at me tomorrow in front of everyone else. Harriet the crazy cat lover.

The problem with that theory was that Mallory looked as though she meant it. She really did think it was cool. That was the most surprising thing. But it was much easier to think of her as a possible spy than as a potential cat-lover and friend.

I put on my most professional voice. "Does your cat have any special requirements, dietary or otherwise? Any special care instructions?"

I'd spent weeks hating Mallory. It was too late to change now.

Blue Streak did go like a blue streak, but it was because he was easily spooked. Rattling blinds, blowing curtains, slamming doors – they all sent him racing for cover, under the sofa, up a tree or back into his cage. The situation wasn't improved by Cleo, who was deeply offended that another Siamese should have invaded her territory. She let herself be stroked and petted, and chased him away if he dared approach for a pat too.

"He should be called Yellow Streak," I told Adam and Ellie. "He's a total coward. And Cleo's such a bully, I think she should take the lead role in your film."

"You can't blame Cleo," Ellie said. "She's missing her home."

"And your uncle," said Adam, from behind his book.

"You can't blame Blue Streak either," Ellie said. "It would get on anyone's nerves, living with Mean Old Mallory and her dad."

"You don't even know them," Adam said. "Don't be unfair."

"I feel like I know them," Ellie said, "from everything Harry has said, and I know that he is a sneaky, slimy bird smuggler—"

"Leaping to conclusions," Adam said.

"And she is the meanest, most—"

"All *right*, Ellie," Adam said.

"As-mean-as-a-pinball-machine," Ellie said quickly.

For a moment I saw Mallory again in my mind's eye (and what kind of stupid phrase is that? You only have two eyes; nobody has a third, hidden one.) In my mind's-eye-that-didn't-exist, Mallory's eyes were glowing. *"This is so cool,"* her voice said. But I shook my head to get rid of it. Ellie was right. Mallory was as mean as a pinball machine. It was no use trying to see her any differently now.

Chapter Twenty-five

AT SCHOOL, MALLORY WAS STILL THE centre of her group, still as mean and undiluted evil as ever, but I sensed her mind was somewhere else. (*Yuck* – portable minds. Imagine that.) Mr Cool kept having to ask her things twice, and she went on about indoor netball as usual, but in a half-hearted sort of way.

Half-hearted. Did that mean the other half of her heart was somewhere else as well? Maybe in the same place where her portable mind had gone?

I knew where. For days, she kept looking at me as though she wanted to know something, but wished she didn't have to ask me. But I wasn't going to help. Why should I make it any easier for her? Finally, she came out with it one lunchtime. Instead of totally ignoring me as usual, she sort of muttered: "How's Blue Streak?"

I was ready for her. I'd already spent an enjoyable morning inventing possible replies:

Totally cowed by Cleo.

Horribly homesick – though I can't imagine why.

Perfectly happy, I shouldn't think he'll ever want to leave.

Sick, but the vet's fairly sure he'll recover. We'll have to add his charges to the bill.

But when I opened my mouth, somehow none of those replies came out. "He's fine," I heard myself say. "He's settling in okay."

I was feeling sorry for Blue Streak, that's what it was. A nice animal, trapped like a cat up a tree in a horrible family. It was nothing to do with the way Mallory had looked at me. The glowing eyes, the awed voice. "*This is so cool.*"

Mallory nodded briefly. Then she pushed past and charged out the door, yelling, "Wait up, you guys! You've got to hear about my new bedroom furniture!"

All my bedroom furniture was second-hand. I felt sorry for Blue Streak, but I wasn't a bit sorry for Mean Mallory Woz-Jingle-Jansky. She was just annoying. And it was even more annoying when she called a meeting of the Recycling Team.

"Who made her the leader?" I grumbled to Callum, as we sat around waiting for everyone else to arrive.

"She'd make a good leader," he said, which was not what I wanted to hear. "But so would you," he added quickly. "You could be co-leaders, if you're going to have a hissy fit about it."

"Excuse me, Callum," I said with dignity. "I do not have hissy fits. When did you ever see me having a hissy fit? Huh? Tell me that? When? When?"

"Uh – right now?" Callum said, edging away.

Mallory had a whole raft of ideas already sorted. The others sat there open-mouthed while ideas just poured out of her. Actually, I'm not sure what a raft of ideas would look like. I hoped they would all sink, but everyone else seemed really keen.

"To start with, we change our name," she announced. "From now on, we aren't the Recycling Team. We're the Futures Team, because" – Callum played an imaginary drum roll on the desks – "we are the Team of the Future."

"Futures Team. Cool," everyone murmured. I didn't say a thing.

Her first idea was a Rubbish Bin Painting Competition, to see which class could do the best job of decorating their rubbish bin.

"Our rubbish bins are scungy!" I declared. "I wouldn't touch them with a bargepole."

"You wouldn't have to," Callum sniggered, while I was still wondering what a bargepole was and where you found one. "You'd be touching them with a paintbrush."

"Whatever. It's a health and safety issue – the teachers wouldn't let us."

"We'll get the caretaker to hose them out. Even better – we'll get the junior classes to," Mallory decided. "It can be part of their water play."

Next was the worm farm. Mallory said that a worm farm was essential, and the kids could line up to feed it their apple cores, orange peels and other biodegradable leftovers.

I don't mind worms. Really, I don't, because I like animals.

Well, maybe I mind them just a little. Worms are slimy and squirmy and … I can't help it … the thought of them makes me feel squirmy too.

"What are you pulling faces for?" Callum asked.

"I am not," I said. "And who's going to pay for all this, anyway? Paints? Brushes? The teachers won't let you just raid the art room. And a worm farm? The worms?"

"We'll go downtown and get the paint shop to donate paints and brushes. The school can pay for the rest," Mallory said airily.

"You mean you're just going to bowl up and ask Mr Bennett to shell out?"

"Pretty much," Mallory agreed. "We are the Team of the Future. It'll be good for the school's profile, and the principal can tell prospective parents that we're eco-friendly. He can't refuse."

Bowling up to the principal and asking for lots of money that he couldn't refuse – I was starting to like this idea a little bit more.

"Perhaps I'd better come too. I know Mr Bennett better than you do."

"So?" said Mallory.

Her next two ideas were equally bizarre: a Giant Garage Sale, and a Tip Trip.

"I've arranged for the little kids to go on a class trip to the rubbish dump," she explained. (Even Callum, who was turning into a bit of a fan, couldn't help sniggering at that.) "I'm going with them. You can come too, if you want."

"No, thanks!" I said, but afterwards I wished I had. Callum went; they got a whole morning off school, and the little kids climbed off the bus grinning their heads off.

"That was so much fun!"

"That was the best trip I've ever been on!"

It was *so* annoying. Even the parents were saying what a fascinating trip it had been. What could be so fascinating about a trip to the tip? I wasn't going to ask, that's for sure.

"Thanks, Mallory!" the kids chorused, and they all high-fived her as they ran off. For days afterwards, you couldn't go anywhere in the playground without tripping over some little kid racing over to see her. "'Scuse-me-where's-Mallory-have-you-seen-her?" they'd gasp in one breath, and then dash off in another direction – if they couldn't find Mallory – towards the worm farm instead.

The paint shop donated masses of tester pots; the rubbish bins looked great and the worm farm was another big success. Mallory was right; Mr Bennett happily shelled out for it. He started including it in his tours for new parents, and he made a special point of feeding it his banana peel every day.

"*I've* got an idea," Callum said proudly. "We'll get people to adopt a worm. They can pay fifty cents a week, and name it, and we'll send them a weekly progress report."

"Oh, like 'this week your worm has died'?"

"No, like 'Today your worm Frank enjoyed a healthy and nutritious lunch of carrot sticks and apple cores. Thank you for continuing to support our eco-friendly school.'"

Even Callum's crazy idea took off. When the kids lined up at the end of lunchtime to feed the worm farm you could hear them yelling, "There's Stanley!" "Hi, Henrietta!"

Being in the Recycling Team was just so much fun. Oh, sorry. The *Futures* Team. Kids kept coming up to ask if they could join our team instead of the one they were stuck in. I sent them off to the principal, hoping they'd interrupt his lunch.

Meanwhile, Jessica's Charities Team plodded on. There was nobody left with any good ideas. All they were doing was Bad Hair Day, which had been done a hundred times before, and they hadn't even managed to convert it into Good Hair Day. ("Bad Hair Day? That'll be easy for Harry," Karl said, "she can come as she is.")

The trouble was, *I* wasn't coming up with any good ideas, either. I was starting to think I'd lost my powers of imagination, and *that* would be a *total* disaster.

Chapter Twenty-six

IT WAS ABOUT NOW THAT I HAD TO GET braces, which didn't help my frame of mind, but it was typical of the year I was having. They try to make you think braces are cool by letting you choose different colours, but that's just a trick to cover up the fact that you're getting a mouthful of metal.

Karl Ballentyne thought it was a huge joke. "No wonder they put you in the Recycling team," he said, *smirk smirk*. "It was so you can recycle all the old drink cans and wire them up inside your mouth. Harriet Wire-fence Waterlily!"

The orthodontist was near Mum's work, so after my appointments I'd call in to see her, and we'd go home on the bus together. Her office was upstairs in an ordinary-looking building. Downstairs was a café, next to a fruit shop and a florist. Inside, a ricketty old lift took you up to the third floor, where you walked past a software company and an ancient-looking dentist's surgery to the door of the law office. Whatever they were spending their ill-gotten gains on (big houses, smart cars, overseas trips), it wasn't expensive office space.

The receptionist, Georgia, had the longest fingernails I'd ever seen, painted bright red like talons, but she was quite nice. I think she was pleased to have someone else to talk to, because she looked pretty bored. She kept a stash of glossy magazines under her desk to leaf through in quiet spells, which seemed to be most of the time.

Sometimes Georgia was off sick. She seemed to have a lot of sick days (maybe she was being gradually poisoned by all the chemicals in her make-up and nail polish) and on those days Mum was always especially glad to see me, because it meant she could pop out to the bank or do some work while I sat at reception.

"You're not going to leave me on my own, are you?" I said, the first time it happened. This must be how Dad felt when he was left in charge of the cats. "What if anyone comes in? I won't know what to say."

"There aren't many appointments booked," Mum said. "Mallory's father is away most of this week, organising the house move, and Mr Page is away at a conference. If someone comes in, just ask them to wait, and come and get me."

Luckily the phone system wasn't too complicated, although I had to mumble a bit to cover the fact that I couldn't pronounce the name of the firm. You'd think they would have realised that having an unpronounceable name mightn't be good for business.

"Do you mind if I pop down to the café for a takeaway latte?" Mum asked. She was halfway out the door before I could say no, but I thought I could cope. The afternoon was nearly over, and Mum looked worn out. A coffee might wake her up a bit.

She left me a pile of letters to open and date-stamp. Working my way through the stack of mail, I suddenly froze. The letter in my hand looked like a bank statement. Nothing strange about that. But the stamp was a Thai one, and the bank's address was in Bangkok – the capital of Thailand.

My heart started to thump. Solid evidence at last! Mr Woz probably kept all his incriminating records in his office. He would have a secret file for them, or a secret safe. I couldn't go and look of course. His office was bound to be locked.

I got up and wandered round the reception area for a bit, as though stretching my legs. Somehow I found myself in front of Mr Woz's door.

It wasn't locked.

I was sure I wasn't supposed to go into his office, but Mum had never actually told me *not* to, and all I was doing was putting some mail on his desk ...

And having a quick look round ...

No sign of a safe. But there was a filing cabinet under the window. All the other files were kept in an alcove off the reception area. So what was in this one? I went round behind the desk, pretending to myself that I was just going to look out the window, but I leant down and pulled at the handle of the top drawer. It stayed shut. I tugged harder.

The door opened behind me, and I whirled round. "Mum! I was just—"

But it wasn't Mum. It was Mr Woz, holding a newspaper and a can of drink. He was wearing casual clothes for once, not a suit and tie, although they were very smart casual clothes. Even his T-shirt looked dry-cleaned and freshly ironed.

And he was looking very surprised to see me in his office. "Harriet?" he said.

I heard myself give a sort of squeak. It sounded as feeble as one of Zoe Watson's squeaks, but I couldn't help it. All I could think was: *Help! I'm in the same room as a dangerous lawyer and wildlife smuggler. Probably with gang connections. And Mum's not here to rescue me!*

"I was just seeing if Mum was coming back," I gabbled, looking out the window for the first time. "She just went out for—" Maybe Mum wasn't supposed to pop out for coffee in work time. She might get fired if I said where she'd gone. "She just—"

Mr Woz looked, too. Unfortunately, his office didn't have a view of the street at all. It stared straight into the windows of another office building ... in fact, straight into the building where my orthodontist worked. There he was, one floor lower down, fiddling round with the wires inside some poor kid's mouth. I wondered which room was worse to be in: my orthodontist's surgery, or Mr Woz's office with Mr Woz in it.

Mr Woz was still looking at me, and I was still holding the Thai bank statement.

"And – um – I was going to put this mail on your desk ..."

Mr Woz held out his hand. It was very clean, and his fingernails were perfectly shaped. Not like Dad's hands, covered in grease and oil, with broken nails and stubby fingers like mine. I passed the envelope across to him, and he inspected it carefully, while I stood there, not daring to move.

"Interested in Thailand, are you?" he said at last.

"Um ..."

"Collect stamps, maybe?"

"Yes!" I grabbed at the suggestion, while sending frantic thought-messages downstairs to the café. *Mum! Get your coffee! Come back*!

More footsteps. Thank goodness, Mum at last. But the footsteps sounded a bit fast for her. Maybe she was panicking that her secret coffee expedition had been found out. I'd have to watch her begging and pleading to keep her job. It would be horrible.

"Dad? Where are you?" A voice rang out in the empty reception area.

No, it was worse than horrible. It wasn't Mum

at all. It was Mallory. "Can we go now? You said you'd only be five minutes, and I've been waiting downstairs for ages." Mallory bowled in through the door, and skidded to a halt, just like Tilda did sometimes. If the whole situation hadn't been so excruciatingly embarrassing, it could almost have been funny.

"Harry! What are *you* doing here?"

Just what I'm wondering myself.

"Harriet was helping out, in Georgia's absence," Mr Woz said smoothly. "Thank you, Harriet. I'll deal with this." He dropped the envelope onto his desk, and I scurried away, face burning, and sank down into the seat at the reception desk.

Phew! Safe at last! I thought. And then, *Oh no! What an idiot*!

I'd blown my cover for sure. Mr Woz must know now that I suspected him. My knees were still trembling. I tried to look busy with the remaining letters. Then I changed my mind and pushed them to the back of the desk, in case they reminded Mr Woz that I'd been going through *his* mail.

They didn't stay long. Mr Woz tossed his empty drink can in the bin and called goodbye. I mumbled something in return without looking up, so I don't know if Mallory looked at me, but she certainly didn't say anything.

Mum didn't seem worried after bumping into them at the lifts, so maybe he hadn't told about finding me in his office, and hopefully she wouldn't get fired.

"Are you all right, Harry? You look a bit flushed. Anyway, Alex said to finish up early as it's Friday, so I'll just tidy up and then we can go."

Maybe Mr Woz hadn't told her, because he was going to keep it hanging over my head, like that Damocles thing Mr Cool once told us about. Damocles had been a happy man until he looked up and saw a sharp sword hanging over his head, suspended by a single horse hair. This filled him with a terrible sense of impending doom.

I could relate to the sense of doom, even without the sword. What if I was going to be blackmailed? What if Mr Woz threatened to say I'd stolen something from his office while I was in there on my own? Exactly what lengths would a dangerous drug dealer go to once he realised he was under suspicion?

Two things were certain: I was going to keep out of his way as much as I could from now on, and *no way* was I *ever* going back into his office.

Chapter Twenty-seven

BEING CAUGHT IN MR WOZ'S OFFICE WAS far worse than being trapped in the aviary. Every time I thought about it, I felt like sinking into the ground. I could just see myself, sinking down, stuck in the mud, while everyone pointed and laughed at me.

My life since kindergarten had featured a whole series of embarrassing events, but this was by far the worst. Only the cats helped, purring and rubbing my legs as though they didn't care a bit about whatever stupid and embarrassing things I'd done.

After a few weeks, Blue Streak went to his new home. It was even bigger and grander now that the renovations were finished. I wondered how Blue Streak would cope when Mr Woz filled the aviaries with smuggled birds; he'd probably be spooked by them, too.

"He's the scaredest cat in the whole world," Ellie said disgustedly.

"I thought you felt sorry for him having to live with Mean Old Mallory."

"I did, but then I stopped, because he's such a scaredy-cat," Ellie said.

I hadn't told her or anyone else about the embarrassing episode at Page, Wotzit & Associate. Astonishingly, neither had Mallory. Either that, or she'd told everyone and sworn them to secrecy, and they were all laughing at me behind my back.

We still hadn't heard from Uncle Theo, not even a postcard. That wasn't particularly surprising, because hardly anyone sends postcards any more. If you're going on holiday nowadays you email, or set up a blog, or you text someone when you're lost in the jungle, so they can organise a rescue for you from the other side of the world. Uncle Theo had an email address, and he was certainly computer literate, but maybe he was worried about dodgy security at Internet cafes, or getting his own computer hacked into.

Or maybe he'd just forgotten his password.

Mum didn't seem too bothered, but I worried that he was lost somewhere in deepest darkest Europe without his passport, money, phone or any travel documents. Philosophy might not be a lot of practical help in such a situation.

I'd decided to email him my Workplace Interview, not that he was *at* his work place, but he's a philosopher so I guess you could say his workplace is his mind. *What is the title of your job … what skills do you need … what training did you have … what subjects would be useful for this type of work?*

If he didn't answer I might have to make up the answers myself, because it was due in soon.

"Harry? You come to my birthday party?" Tina asked shyly.

"Is it your birthday, Tina? Sure, I'd love to come. When is it?"

"Tomorrow night," Tina said. "Saturday." She didn't have proper invitations or anything, but she wrote down her address on a piece of paper. "Five o'clock, okay?"

"Okay," I said. It felt like I hadn't been to anyone's birthday party for ages.

"Is only small party," Tina said. "I only ask two people."

"That doesn't matter. Who's the other person?"

"Mallory," Tina said happily.

"Mallory? You're asking Mallory and me to your party?"

"Yes," Tina said.

I took a breath and let it out slowly. "O-kay."

"You still can come?" Tina said anxiously.

I opened my mouth to make up an excuse, something I'd suddenly remembered I was doing on Saturday night. Then I stopped, because two sides of me were having a fight inside my head, and I really wasn't sure which side was going to win.

One side said, *You can't say no, you just told Tina you'd come.*

The other side said, But I don't want to go, if Mallory is the only other guest.

Tina asked you specially.

Yeah, me and Mallory.

So? She wants you to come.

I got the feeling the birthday side was winning. The opposition made a last desperate effort: But it's only a small party. No proper invites or anything.

Tina will be really disappointed if you don't turn up.

"Harry," Tina said, "why are you making all those funny faces?"

"Nothing," I said. "Sure, Tina. Of course I can come."

The boys were climbing all over the desks at the end of lunchtime, pretending to be circus acrobats. Karl was being a clown, which wasn't hard, seeing as he was a clown most of the time anyway.

"Hey, Mallory, want to come for a sleepover tomorrow night?" I heard Jessica ask.

Mallory shook her head. "Sorry. Can't. Busy."

Me too, I thought. But did Mallory know I was going? And if she did, did she know that before or after she accepted Tina's invite?

Chapter Twenty-eight

I THOUGHT I WAS GOING TO BE LATE, because I lost the piece of paper with Tina's address. But we got there just as Mallory was climbing out of the car.

"Do you know where you're going?" Dad said. Then: "Is that Mallory? The two of you will be all right together, won't you?"

That was a question that was impossible to answer, so I didn't bother trying. "Bye," I said. "I'll ring when I need a lift home."

Tina lived in an apartment block, with one of those security phones where you punch in a number and wait to be let in. We stood in front of it, not talking. Mallory pushed the numbers.

I looked sideways at her present. She looked sideways at mine.

I love wrapping up presents. Mallory's present was flat and rectangular, and her 'Happy 13th Birthday' card was big and expensive-looking. Hers might have cost more, but mine looked way more beautiful. I'd cut out silver stars to scatter over purple wrapping paper, and tied it with ruby-red ribbon, and made a card by gluing hundreds and thousands onto a heart shape.

Nobody answered. Mallory hit the numbers again, and this time the buzzer went.

"Hello?" a fuzzy voice said.

Mallory leaned forward. "We're here for Tina's birthday party," she said clearly.

The buzzer squawked again and the door clicked open. We went into the lobby, not talking, and waited for the lift. When it arrived, we got in silently. Mallory hit the button for the fifth floor. The door closed, but nothing happened. The lift didn't move.

It felt very silly, standing in a tiny space, not moving, and not saying anything.

"How was your netball game this morning?" I said at last, not looking at her.

"Walkover," Mallory said, not looking at me.

The lift doors opened again. We were still on

the ground floor. An old lady with a walking stick got in and pressed one of the buttons on the panel. The doors shut, but the lift still didn't move. The old lady clucked in annoyance.

"Not again! Ridiculous! I must speak to the management." She thumped the panel with her walking stick, and the lift jerked into movement. At the first floor it stopped again, and she got out without looking at either of us and stomped off to her apartment.

Mallory still didn't speak, but she giggled quietly to herself. Then we were at the fifth floor, and Tina was waiting with a big smile on her face.

"Hi, Tina. Happy birthday!" Mallory said, handing over her present.

"Thank you," Tina said, but when she saw mine, her eyes widened. "Oh, so pretty!"

There was a neat row of shoes lined up by the front door. Mallory bent down to undo the gleaming white laces on her smart new running shoes.

Uh-oh. I knew what was going to be under those smart new running shoes. Smart new socks, with no holes in them.

"You have to take your shoes off!" Mallory hissed.

"I *know* that," I muttered, pulling them off without bothering to undo my broken-and-knotted-together laces. My socks *always* had holes in them. I twisted my sock so the hole was underneath, and followed Tina and Mallory inside.

The apartment was very small, and full of spicy cooking smells. Tina's mum was busy in the kitchen, and her dad and little sister and someone else – a neighbour, maybe, or an aunt – were sitting in the lounge. Her sister was watching TV, and her dad told her in another language to turn it off. I said hello, but she was too shy to answer.

The three of us squeezed onto the sofa, Tina in the middle. My big toe was wiggling its way out of my sock. I bent down and pretended to scratch my ankle while I tugged the hole back out of sight.

Tina beamed at us, but I wasn't sure what we were going to do next.

"Aren't you going to open your presents?" Mallory asked.

Hers was an illustrated book about endangered animals, with a tiger on the cover. It was a good choice for Tina, whose English isn't perfect. The book got passed around. Her dad and the neighbour pointed to the pictures, smiling and admiring them.

Tina didn't want to unwrap my present. She turned it over and over, tracing the silver stars and stroking the ribbon. But when she did open it, she loved it. I'd bought her a stationery set, all pink: pink notebook and pens and pencils, a pink pencil sharpener and stapler, even pink Sellotape. She took everything out and we looked at it – her little sister gradually edging nearer and nearer – and all the time I was thinking, *What do we do now?*

"What do we do now?" Tina said happily, as though she didn't realise she was supposed to provide the entertainment. There was no sign of any games. No balloons, no streamers, no party stuff at all, except for a cake, and even that didn't have any candles.

"Um – we could look at your stuff in your bedroom," I said. Tina looked blank. "Don't you have things we can look at? Photos and stuff?"

Her little sister followed us in and sat on one of the beds. We sat in a row on the other. I tugged at my sock again.

"I show you my photos from home," Tina said, pulling out a photo album. "This, my grandma – this my cousin – this my other cousin – my aunty—"

"You must have a big family," Mallory said.

"I bet you miss them all."

"Yes, miss them very much," Tina said simply. Her cousins and aunts and uncles smiled back at us. The flowers and houses in the background looked so different from ours; it must be strange for Tina here, where everything felt normal and ordinary to us.

Her mum called us downstairs. There was a proper tablecloth on the table, and paper napkins, and the table was laden with food: bowls of noodles and bowls of sauces, mini samosas, puffed up chippie things, plates of chopped up vegetables and hard-boiled eggs, and other things I couldn't even recognise.

"Help yourself," Tina's mum said, smiling and holding out plates. "Come, eat, eat."

"Thank you," said Mallory politely. She took very small helpings and ate slowly, but I thought it was delicious. I forgot about the hole in my sock, and went back for seconds and then thirds. Tina's mum smiled and smiled.

"You like? You like?" she kept saying. "Have more, more!"

Tina chattered away nonstop with her family, switching to English with us. It was amazing to listen to. At school we were used to her talking so haltingly, always searching for the right word, or getting the grammar wrong.

I could hardly move when it was time to go. Quite possibly I wouldn't fit inside the lift again. I would have to stay with Tina's family forever, and live on rice and noodles.

Mallory bent down and did up her smart new running shoes, but I held mine dangling by their broken laces. Tina took us back to the lift, her sister trailing behind.

"Thank you for coming," she said.

"Thank you for coming," chirped her little sister, and then she quickly hid behind Tina.

"Thanks, Tina. Great party," Mallory said.

The lift doors closed. Nothing happened. The lift didn't move.

I looked sideways at Mallory. She was looking sideways at me.

"Not again! Ridiculous! I must speak to the management," she said, thumping the panel. The lift jerked again and started to move. Both of us burst out laughing.

"Oh, don't make me laugh, I'm so full," I groaned.

We were actually talking to each other like normal people, but as soon as we stepped out of the lift, things felt awkward again. Her dad's car was already waiting.

"Give you a lift home, if you like," Mallory said.

No way. "It's okay. I already phoned home."

"Oh. Well. Bye, then," Mallory said. Her dad didn't say hello or smile or anything. Maybe because I was holding my shoes in one hand, with my toe sticking out through the hole in my sock, or maybe he was remembering our last meeting. They pulled away just as our car drew up behind.

"Good party?" Dad said.

"Kind of," I said. Kind of ironic, was what it was. Mallory had *almost* seemed likeable for once, but how could I like someone whose father was totally mean and nasty and horrible? He was almost definitely a criminal. He was almost certainly going to prison.

It was way too late to start liking her now. Of course it was.

Wasn't it?

Chapter Twenty-nine

"GREAT PARTY, TINA," I SAID ON Monday morning. Tina beamed and held out a plastic container full of fried noodles.

"My mum give this to you, for your lunch," she said.

"Oh, yum, thanks!" I said, and then Mr Cool came in.

Here we go. The start of yet another wildly exciting week. I tune out at school whenever anyone says "sport". (This means I spend a lot of time tuned out. Some days I might as well stay home.) So it was only afterwards that I realised Mr Cool must have said "Sports" and "Exchange."

I tuned back in when he said "St Benedict's."

The classroom had erupted into a lava-flow of cheers, shouts and questions. St Benedict's? Wasn't that where Ellie (and sometimes Adam) went? Hadn't Ellie mentioned some sort of Sports Exchange? She'd been looking forward to it, but I thought it sounded boring. Worse than boring. I wouldn't even be able to sit at my desk, doodling cat pictures on my refill pad. No matter how much Mr Cool dressed it up with talk about "interschool cooperation", it was still just sport. Netball, soccer, rugby and hockey. And that meant I'd have to stand around outside for hours, watching balls being thrown or kicked or hit around, and being deafened by everyone else's cheers and yells.

"I'm hoping everyone will take part in at least one sporting activity," Mr Cool said, looking straight at me.

"Not Harry," Karl said. "We want to win, remember."

I crushed him with a withering glance. "I don't *do* sport, remember?" Then I turned back to Mr Cool. "I'll be the official artist, if you like."

Mr Cool's eyebrows did their quizzical thing. "Official artist? I hadn't thought of having one of those."

"You don't have to," I said. "I've thought of

it for you. They have official war artists … and sport is kind of like war, isn't it?" There were several pictures that I would enjoy drawing, such as Ellie knocking Mallory out with a hockey stick, and a St Benedict's soccer player sidestepping round Karl Ballentyne for a goal. Ellie said their soccer team hadn't lost a game all season.

She was so excited that afternoon. "We're coming to play you at sport! It's going to be the most fun time I've ever had, and we get to meet Mallory the Meanie, close up. I bet your school is heaps more fun than ours."

"I wouldn't count on it. Your school sounds more fun to me. Do you think we could swap?" School, the way it used to be before Mallory came along and spoiled it all, including my best ever best-friendship with Jessica.

Although maybe, just maybe it wasn't Mallory's fault. Jessica was so into labels and designer gear these days, for everything from T-shirts and baseball caps to bags and wallets and lip gloss. Sometimes I had a niggling suspicion that Jessica, not Mallory, would have fitted better into that picture that Mr Cool had confiscated, wailing about her Roxy handbag. If we were planets, Jessica would have moved into a different solar system by now. We just weren't in the same orbit any more.

"I bet you'll beat us at everything," Ellie went on, "but we might beat you at a few things. We might beat you at hockey."

Quite possibly, if Ellie was playing. I could imagine her charging round the field, furiously wielding a hockey stick. She'd be fearless.

"What sport are you playing?" she asked.

"I don't do sport. I'm being official artist."

"We've invited Adam to be on our team. He's playing chess," Ellie said.

I looked over his shoulder at his book, which was full of black-and-white diagrams. "Mr C—Mr Cameron didn't say anything about chess."

"It's on the notice," Ellie said. "Maybe your teacher didn't think anyone could play."

"Doesn't matter," Adam said. "I can set up a board and play against myself."

"No, no! You can play me!" I said. "That'll be much more fun than standing round watching boring sports games."

Ellie looked hurt. "*Hockey* isn't going to be boring," she said.

"Of course not, Ellie," I said quickly. "Hockey is going to be wildly exciting and quite possibly dangerous."

"Can you play chess?" Adam said doubtfully.

"No. Can you teach me?"

Ellie ran back home to get Adam's chess set. The cats curled inquisitively around us while Adam set it up. He explained what all the pieces were and how they could move, but I soon got lost. When he said, "Move one of your pawns," I had no idea what to do.

"Which ones are the prawns, again? I mean pawns?"

Even Ellie knew that. She pointed them out to me. Living with someone who knew everything seemed to have distinct advantages, such as the fact that some of his knowledge rubbed off on you almost without noticing.

"This is so hard," I complained. "There are too many different options."

"Four hundred possibilities for the first two moves," Adam said. "We each have eight pawns, which can move one space or two, and two knights which can move in one of two directions. That makes twenty possible moves each, and twenty times twenty is four hundred."

I nearly gave up right there and then.

"Adam could *tell* you which pieces to move," Ellie said.

"But I want people to think I *can* play. I want

them to think I'm incredibly smart."

There was a pause, during which I couldn't help noticing that neither of them said, "But you *are* incredibly smart."

Then Ellie hopped up and down excitedly. "I know! You need a secret code. A signal for each piece, like ..." She thought for a moment. "... like Adam could touch his chin for the Queen, or his ear for the King. And he could point which direction with one hand, and tap out how many squares to move."

"Ellie, you're brilliant," I said.

"Not all the time," Ellie said modestly. "I'm only brilliant in bursts. I think that must have been one of the bursts."

"Although it is *sort* of cheating."

"No, it's a creative way of sharing information," Ellie said.

"Splitting hairs," Adam said, studying a chess game in his book.

He got the code straightaway but it took me longer to put the gestures and taps together. We made up a few more signals: I ran my fingers through my hair for *repeat the signal*. If Adam coughed as I went to move a piece, that meant *don't do that!* And some pieces can only move in one direction, so he didn't always need to point.

"What happens if I end up playing someone else?"

"You won't," Adam said. "I'm the only one playing."

"Are you going to let me win?" I asked, but Adam just smiled.

"He's got a killer instinct when he plays chess," Ellie said. "He never lets *anyone* win."

It took a lot of practice, not helped by Tilda pouncing on the chessboard and scattering the pieces. Adam made me memorise the first ten moves of several different games. After that, he'd start directing me.

"Let's go, Ellie," he said at last. "We've been here for ages. Harry will be sick of us."

"No she won't be," Ellie said. "We've been very helpful, plus I had a brilliant flash of intuition which has saved her from ridicule on the sports field."

That sounded like something I might have said. It was nice to have a friend with a good vocabulary and a bit of imagination. The only trouble was, Ellie was heaps younger than me. Mallory showed sparks of imagination sometimes, but . . .

But, nothing. Mallory was Mallory, after all.

On the Friday before the Sports Exchange, everyone was supposed to be signed up for whatever sports they wanted to play.

"I'll sort out the lists over lunchtime," Mr Cool said. "You might not be able to do everything you've put down for, because some of the matches are on at the same time."

Groans of disappointment.

"Can't we spread it out over two days instead?" Karl called out.

"No," said Mr Cool. "There's the small matter of the curriculum, which we have to cover as well as sport." (Who would have guessed?)

"Can't we just miss out something else, like maths?" Callum said.

"An innovative suggestion, Callum, but ultimately unworkable."

"Does that mean yes or no?" Callum whispered to Karl.

"Can't we schedule them *all* for the same time?" I said. "Then it would be over sooner."

"No," said Mr Cool. "Now, has everyone put their name down for something? Harry – apart from being official artist?"

"Harry doesn't do sport," called a chorus of voices.

"Yes, I have. I'm down for chess," I said.

"Chess?" Jessica said. "I didn't know you could play chess."

Mr Cool looked down at his lists. "You're right, St Benedict's do have a chess team, although" – he looked closer – "there's only one person in it. Adam Buckler."

"That's all right," I said. "I'll play him."

Zoe was sitting at her desk, looking suddenly uncertain. She hadn't cottoned onto the chess option either. Nobody seemed to have. "Maybe I should do chess, too," she said.

"Good idea, Zoe," a chorus of voices called out, from everyone who didn't want her on their sports team.

"Are you going to be umpiring it, Mr Cameron?" Zoe asked.

"Me? No, I'll be busy down on the sportsfield," Mr Cool said. "I think we'll have to leave it to Harry and, ah, Adam to regulate their own game."

"Oh, well, perhaps I won't," Zoe decided, to another chorus of disappointed groans.

"All right, then," said Mr Cool, obviously having difficulty adjusting to the idea of me being involved in a sporting event. Not that chess really counted as a sport. "Does that mean you won't be the official artist after all, Harry? I didn't know you could play chess. Perhaps you could set up a chess club at lunchtime."

"I don't think many people would be interested," I said. "Chess takes brains, not brawn." *Brawn*. Another lovely word. It sounded like some disgusting mess that you'd see on the meat counter at the supermarket; exactly the right term for sports-crazy people like ...

Karl Ballentyne choked into the sports drink he wasn't supposed to be drinking in class. "So why are *you* playing it?" he said.

"Isn't that obvious?" I said.

"I'll have that, thank you, Karl," Mr Cool said, with his pen hovering over the team lists. "Right, then, Harry – chess."

Chapter Thirty

MR COOL HAD SAID THE EXCHANGE would go ahead rain, hail, snow or sunshine. It didn't worry me what the weather did, seeing as chess was an indoor activity, but everyone else was worried. The whole class – except me – was lined up by the windows on Monday morning, deeply involved in a pointless debate about whether or not it was going to rain. Pointless, because either it was going to rain or it wasn't, and talking about it wasn't going to change anything.

"It can't rain," Jessica wailed. "I bought these new shorts specially."

"I don't think the weather forecast is connected

to your credit card," I said, but I don't think anyone heard.

Or maybe Mallory did. She was smiling at something, anyhow.

We could hear the St Benedict's kids coming from several streets away. It was grey and cloudy, but not actually raining, when they came trooping in with their teachers at half past nine. Adam was right at the back, carrying his chess set under one arm, and reading as he walked. They lined up in the playground, and so did we. Ellie waved frantically to me and mouthed "Where is she?" Mallory was deep in discussion with Jessica, Claudine and Aleesha; probably swotting up some last-minute netball strategies. I pointed her out. Ellie's mouth made a wide "O".

"What are you pointing at?" Karl said behind me.

"Nothing. Nobody," I said hastily. "There was a bee, that's all. I was waving it away."

"Yeah, you wouldn't want a bee to get into your hair, would you?" Karl said. "Then you'd really have a bee in your bonnet." He and Callum went off, bashing each other's arms and laughing, as though he'd said something clever for once.

Mr Cool directed the chaos from the middle of the playground, dividing everyone into teams and sending them off to the right place. I waited for Zoe to sigh, "So cool and decisive!" but she wasn't even looking at him. She was looking at ... "Who's that tall guy over there?"

"That's A—" I started to say, but luckily other voices broke in first. After all, the whole point was that I wasn't supposed to know who Adam was. I'd almost let the cat out of the bag right at the start. (And why is that a bad thing to do? Some cats, like Tilda, just like climbing into bags. Or boxes, or cupboards – and you don't want them to stay trapped in there forever, do you?)

"The one with the book?" Aleesha.

"He's really good-looking, don't you think?" Zoe again.

"He might be. Hard to tell. Wish he'd look up." Jessica this time.

"Wonder what sport he's going to be playing?"

"I've heard about him. He's like some total genius." That was Claudine.

Genius, yes. But good-looking? What a joke.

Or was it? He did have those amazing blue eyes. I wished I could be around when he turned them on one of the MCAS girls. They might have to regroup as the ABAS.

Eventually the playground was cleared of everyone except Mr Cool, Adam and me. The MCAS girls went off reluctantly. "Oh, no," I heard one of them say. "He must be playing chess – with Harry. What a waste!"

"Right, then," said Mr Cool. "Are you Adam? This is Harry." Adam nodded politely, pretending he didn't know me either. "We've got a table ready for you in the school library. The librarian will supervise, but we've told the other Exchange players that they can come and watch you, if they're not playing anything themselves."

I was good at setting up the chessboard by now. I laid out all the pieces while Mr Cool, Adam and Ms Plott (our librarian) watched.

"Good luck, both of you," Mr Cool said. "I'd better go and start the soccer game."

Adam put the timer he used for each turn on the table, while still reading. I had the secret code scribbled down on a scrap of paper. 'Qch' meant Adam would touch his chin if I was to move my Queen, 'Ke' meant his ear for my King, and so on. The paper was scrunched up in my pocket for emergencies, but hopefully nobody could decipher it, even if I lost it or dropped it by mistake.

"Right, then," I said. "Shall we start?"

Ms Plott was still hovering round. "Can you really play chess? You must both be very clever. I should go and cover some books, but it's fascinating, isn't it? What's that piece called again?"

Adam gave her a slightly surprised look. Our librarian is a bit surprising if you haven't met her before. She's very nice, but she talks so much that sometimes we feel like telling her to be quiet, which is a bit of a reversal if you think of what libraries are supposed to be like, except that our library isn't like that at all.

Adam wasn't answering, so I had to, and it was too hard to talk and remember the code at the same time. If she'd only go away, we could stop playing. It seemed a waste to use our secret code when there was nobody else there to fool.

"I'm sure we've got some good books somewhere on chess," Ms Plott said. "Now what Dewey number would they be under, I wonder? I'll go and check on the computer."

I kicked Adam under the table. "Can we stop? We can start again if anyone comes in."

"Here we are," Ms Plott called from behind a row of shelves. "Oh, dear, no, that's backgammon. I'll keep looking, shall I? Oh, and look, here's that book on dinosaurs that's been missing for months. Now, how did that end up in the games section?"

Ms Plott pottered away happily among the shelves while Adam read and I looked out the window. Every so often a muddy, chattering group would appear in the playground and we'd quickly resume playing positions in case some of them came in to watch. One or two of them did, but the code worked fine. We played a couple of games twice over. Adam won all of them, but I didn't mind. It was a nice, peaceful morning, and it was much better than standing around watching boring netball or soccer.

The problems started with the rain.

Chapter Thirty-one

IT WAS ONLY LIGHT DRIZZLE AT FIRST, BUT the showers soon got heavier.

"Oh, dear," Ms Plott trilled, "look at the rain! That's no good, is it, although the boys won't care, I'm sure, and maybe it will ease off soon." She stood on tiptoes to look out the windows along the back wall. Ms Plott is so short that she always has to stand on a ladder to reach the highest shelves, if there's nobody tall like Karl Ballentyne around to help reach things down for her. She's so short that you often don't realise she's on the other side of a bay of shelves, which can lead to some embarrassing moments if you're in the middle of a private discussion.

"Yes, there they are, still running round in the mud," she said. "It doesn't look like they're calling the netball off just yet, either ... oh, dear, the court must be getting a bit slippery ... oops! There goes someone for a tumble—"

"Hope it's Mallory," I muttered, moving a piece. Adam coughed. I thought he meant *don't be rude,* until I remembered that a cough was also our signal for *don't do that*.

"Oops," I said, rescuing my bishop. "Actually, what I meant to move was ..."

The rain got heavier still and they did call off the netball, with twenty minutes to go till lunchtime, which meant that nearly all the girls came rushing up the stairs into the library and crowded around us. Around Adam, anyway.

"Chess is a fascinating game," Ms Plott was busy telling everyone. "And an ancient game, too, of course. You might like to look at some of these books on moves and strategy. Not that one – that's a book on dinosaurs that I've just found."

"Moves and strategy?" Jessica sounded almost interested.

"Don't get too excited," Aleesha told her. "Not those sort of moves. Not that sort of strategy."

"Rugby's finished!" Claudine yelled from over

by the window, and not long afterwards, a crowd of rugby spectators came thundering in as well.

"What's this?" said voices at the back. "What's going on?"

"Ssh!" said voices at the front. "It's Harry and some boy," said someone from our school.

"It's Adam and some girl," said someone from their school.

"It's Harry and Adam," said some super-intelligent person, putting the two names together.

"Looks pretty boring," said Karl Ballentyne. "When do we cheer? Who's winning?"

"You can't tell till the end," said Ellie. "Don't you know anything?"

There were a few stifled giggles. *Go, Ellie!* I thought.

"Yeah, well, that's pretty hopeless if you ask me," Karl said. "When you're playing a game, you want to know who's winning, don't you?"

"I expect my brother is," Ellie said.

"Yeah, probably," Karl said. "Wouldn't expect Harry to be winning anything."

"Shut up, you'll put them off," said another voice. *Thanks, Mallory!* I thought in amazement. Karl looked surprised too; he always assumed I was the only girl who found him a total pain.

Not that it made any difference to Adam, who hardly seemed to notice anyone else was there. He nudged my foot, reminding me that it was my turn. I looked at my watch. Still more than ten minutes to go till the bell.

"We won the netball," Claudine whispered to Aleesha.

"So? We won the hockey," Ellie said loudly, "*and* the soccer."

"We won the rugby, easy," Karl bragged.

"That means we've won two things and so've they," said Callum, after taking a moment to work it out.

"Hey," Matt said, "that means the chess is the deciding factor. Whichever school wins this has won the Exchange."

"Great," Karl said, "that means we've lost."

This was *really* off-putting. Adam rubbed his nose. I went to move my knight but he coughed. I froze with my hand on the piece. What was wrong with that move? Wasn't that what Adam had signalled – his nose for my knight? He coughed again. And again.

"Sorry," he gasped at last, eyes watering. "Frog in my throat."

I had a sudden vision of a bright green frog leaping out of Adam's mouth and hopping about under the library shelves. Lots of girls would start screaming, and they would all try to climb onto Ms Plott's library ladder, which would collapse under the weight, and someone would break an arm or a leg. It wouldn't be Mallory, though. I couldn't imagine her screaming just because of a cute green frog.

It was the frog that did it. All the secret code flew out of my head, and there was no way I could consult my hidden piece of paper with so many people standing round. I made my next move completely at random. Adam looked puzzled.

"Hey," said Ellie, "you weren't supposed to move that!"

"What do you mean, she wasn't *supposed* to?" said Mallory.

"This is a dumb game," said Jessica. "Come on, let's go and ... *mumble mumble ...*" A group of girls drifted away and started chatting up some of the St Benedict's rugby boys, over by the fiction shelves. *Phew*. But I still couldn't remember how the code went. Adam shrugged and gave up on it too. I was just hanging out for the bell to go, when—

"She's won," Mallory said.

"Who's won?"

"Harry."

"She can't have," Ellie said. "Nobody ever beats Adam."

"She can't have," Karl said. "Harry never wins anything."

But Mallory insisted. "Look, that's not just 'check', it's 'checkmate'."

I could hardly believe it, but it was true. Adam couldn't believe it either. After the bell went, and nearly everyone else charged off, he examined the board for a long time, picking up the pieces one by one and putting them back carefully in the exact same place.

"How did you do that?"

"Beginner's luck?" I offered.

Adam shook his head. "A temporary aberration."

"Well done, Harry," Ellie said, pounding me on the back. "That was nearly as good as us winning the hockey. I got two goals. That Aleesha player's good though. She's almost as good as me."

"Boasting, Ellie," Adam said, finally starting to pack up the pieces.

"No," Ellie said, "telling the truth."

"Do you three know each other, then?" *Oops.* Nearly everyone else had charged off, but not

Mallory. She was turning over the pages of a book on Ms Plott's display shelf.

"Uh … well …" I started, but it was Adam who saved the situation.

He wandered over and picked up another book – the dinosaur one that Ms Plott had found in the wrong place – but he didn't open it. "So, do you play chess?" he asked, looking straight at Mallory with his amazing, clear blue eyes.

"A bit," Mallory said. "My dad tried to teach me once. He's really good at it."

Great. I was trying to work out whether Mallory thought I could play chess, or whether she knew I couldn't. Either way I was sunk, because she'd realise I'd fluked or cheated my way to a win.

Had it been a fluke, or was it the Ellie-and-Adam effect? Had some of Adam's encyclopaedic knowledge of chess rubbed off on me, just by proximity to a genius?

Ellie was shaking her head furiously behind Mallory's back and mouthing "no!" and "don't talk to her!" at Adam, but he was ignoring her.

"Give you a game sometime if you like," he offered. *Thanks, Adam.* Wasn't this fraternising with the enemy? But Adam and Mallory were already walking ahead of us downstairs. Adam still had the dinosaur book in his hand.

"I don't get it," Ellie said. "Adam never talks to girls. And what's he talking to *her* for? Doesn't he know that she's as mean as a pinball machine?"

"Do you think she is?" I asked. Suddenly I wasn't quite sure.

"Well, of course," Ellie said. "You said so. Didn't you?"

Chapter Thirty-two

ST BENEDICT'S RECKONED THEY'D WON THE Sports Exchange, because if you tallied up the points on either side, counting my final chess victory as 1-0 (to us), they'd scored the most points overall. But the North Park kids (well, the ones who were interested – which didn't include me) reckoned we'd won, because it was three wins (rugby, netball and chess) against two (hockey and soccer). Then the St Benedict's kids said chess didn't count, because Adam wasn't officially part of their school.

Mr Bennett said it didn't matter, because it was 'taking part' that was important.

"You don't believe that rubbish though, do

you, Mr Cameron?" asked Karl. "Of course it matters, doesn't it?"

Zoe, for once, wasn't hanging on Mr Cool's every word. "Will you teach me how to play chess, Harry?" she asked. "Do you happen to know if that Adam guy belongs to a chess club?"

I was sure Zoe Watson was not in the slightest bit interested in chess. Then Mallory appeared behind me.

"No," she said calmly. "I happen to know that he doesn't."

We'd finished Conservation at last and we had a new topic: Walls of the World. The boys appeared to get very excited about this until they realised it was 'Walls' and not 'Wars'. We had to draw the walls that we'd studied on a world map, but I hadn't got to that point yet. I was too busy filling in the oceans with a pattern of whales and dolphins, even though I knew what Mr Cool would say. *Harry, presentation is important but it isn't everything. Content matters too, remember?*

So far, we'd done the Great Wall of China, the Gaza Strip, and the North-South Divide in Korea. We'd seen pictures of the Vietnam Veterans' Memorial Wall in Washington DC. We'd studied Hadrian's Wall, built by the Romans to keep the

Scots out, and a fence in a local wildlife sanctuary, built to keep pests out.

The underlying theme seemed to be that Walls were a Bad Thing and they split up families and divided people from each other – apart from the fence in the wildlife sanctuary, which was a Good Thing, because it meant the wildlife didn't get eaten by the pests. (Probably it was a Bad Thing for the pests, who must get hungry and frustrated.) Most of us got the point in five minutes, but we had to go on studying Walls for weeks.

At least Ellie admired my map. "That is so cool, I didn't know you could draw like that," she said. "You must be almost as clever as Adam."

Adam leaned over to have a look as well.

"Interesting place to put the Great Wall of China," he commented.

We sat through a whole day of the principal showing us the digital photos of his trip to Turkey, or maybe it was only an hour, but it felt like a whole day. Most of the photos were of various ruins. You couldn't even *see* the walls of Ancient Troy, because they aren't there any more, but Mr Bennett kept on pointing out on the screen where they *would* have been, if they hadn't fallen down.

He also told us a lot of other boring stuff about

the history of Turkey, which we didn't really want to know. When he got fed up with Karl and Callum talking, he told them that when they grew up and went to Gallipoli, they would wish they'd listened to him so they knew what they were looking at.

"Is Troy in Gallipoli?" Karl said.

"No, you meathead, Gallipoli's in Troy," Callum said.

Mr Bennett said he gave up, and he left, thank goodness. We all cheered Karl and Callum when he'd gone. Luckily Mr Cool was checking sports equipment in the P.E. shed, on the other side of the playground, and he thought they were thank-you cheers for the principal, not for Karl and Callum. Or maybe he was pretending to think that. I noticed he hadn't hung around to watch a million photos of ancient ruins.

Afterwards I thought that we should have pretended to be fascinated by his photos, because the more time Mr Bennett spent in places like Gallipoli, the less time he would spend at school. Perhaps if I left some cruise ship brochures lying around the office, he might go off on a world cruise for a few years. Mr Cool could step in as Acting Principal – no, that wouldn't work, too much sport. The Leadership Teams could take over! After all, there can't be that much to running a school. The teachers do most of the work.

I picked up a handful of cruise ship brochures when we went into town to stock up on cat food again. That was when I spotted the posters in the window of Bonanza Books, next door to the travel agents. *Latest Connor O'Connor on sale now,* they read. *Another Connor O'Connor bestseller! Get your Connor O'Connor books signed here.*

Friday 4.00 pm was handwritten in black ink over a picture of Connor O'Connor himself, surrounded by a menagerie of animals and leading a miniature horse on a rope.

Connor O'Connor is one of Mum's and my favourite authors. We get all his books out from the library, and we've bought a few from second-hand bookshops and school fairs. He lives on his own private island with no other people, just animals, and he writes about the funny things that happen there.

His latest book, *Sweet as Candy,* was on display inside. I flipped through the pages, looking at the photographs and giggling quietly over some of the funny bits. Candy was the name of the miniature horse on the posters. It would be the perfect birthday present for Mum – and even better to get it signed by the author himself.

Dad said he'd take me there, and Mum was very envious that we were going to meet the One and Only Connor O'Connor. I didn't tell her I was buying his latest book for her birthday, but I did hunt out the books we already owned. Once I'd rubbed out the pencilled-in price on the first page, you could hardly tell they were second-hand.

"Can we ask him to sign these, do you think?"

"I'm sure you can. He won't mind, he sounds friendly enough in his books, doesn't he?"

Ha. Little did we know.

Dad picked me up from school and we went straight to Bonanza Books. We got there far too early, so Dad went off to an auto repairs store while I hung around, waiting.

I was standing at the back of the shop when Connor O'Connor himself swept past, preceded by a flustered bookshop assistant. I was pretty sure it was him, although he didn't look nearly as good-looking as he did in his photographs, and I took half a step forward, in case he might sign my books right away.

But then I stepped back again, quickly. Connor O'Connor, who was so funny in his books, was complaining loudly about everything.

"That lunch! Dreadful!" He shuddered in disgust. "And move those posters in the window, they're not visible enough." There had been too many people at one signing, too few at another, his hotel was bad, the weather was bad, the car was uncomfortable, this was a lousy book tour …

The assistant took him into a back room and shut the door, but I could still hear his voice whining on. "Who's in charge here? Didn't you get the list of my requests? I specified a jug of cold water with lemon, and a packet of plain rice crackers." The room was too small, he hadn't had a decent cup of coffee all day, nobody seemed to appreciate what an important bestselling author he was …

Ten minutes later, he emerged (followed by the bookshop assistant in tears) and sat down at the table that had been prepared for him. Straightaway, he seemed to turn into a different person. He switched on a smile and started chatting and signing books.

A queue had already formed, and halfway down I spotted Mallory, clutching a brand-new copy of *Sweet as Candy*. She looked as surprised to see me as I was to see her.

"What are *you* doing here?" she said. "Have

you bought the book? Have you had it signed already?"

The queue shuffled forward a few more paces, but it was moving slowly because Connor O'Connor was chatting so cheerfully to all the people ahead of her.

"Not yet," I said. "Do you like his stuff, then?"

Mallory's face lit up the way I'd only seen it once before. "I love them! I read them over and over – I've bought them all."

Bought, not *borrowed*. Mallory's family obviously didn't need to use libraries. Maybe they didn't know such things existed. It put me off her again.

She turned over the books that I was now holding upside down, in case Connor O'Connor saw them. I thought now he probably had some inbuilt second-hand book sensor. He would be able to recognise their origin from five metres away, and would say something so loud and embarrassing that I'd never dare go back to Bonanza Books ever again.

"Yeah, I've read all of those," Mallory said. "And I can't wait to read this one."

The queue inched forward.

"So why isn't Jessica with you?" I asked.

"Jessica? Come on," Mallory said. "She doesn't read books."

I nearly said "So what does she read? Cornflake packets?" Then I nearly got offended on my ex-best friend's behalf, but when I thought about it, Mallory was right. Jessica read magazine articles about celebrities, diets, and how to get, keep or get rid of a boyfriend, but books bored her. Whenever we had silent reading, she couldn't manage the silent bit, and she never got beyond the first few pages.

"I guess you're right," I said. "She's not a big reader."

Mallory gave a sort of snort. "She's not even a little reader."

I nearly snorted too. If anyone else had said that, I'd have thought it was quite funny. "Well, actually, I'm not buying it. I used to like his books, but I've gone off them."

"Why?" Mallory sounded genuinely curious.

I lowered my voice. "I heard him before, out the back – he's not a bit like he comes across in the books. He's rude and nasty and" – I waved my hands around, trying to express exactly how unpleasant he was – "I wouldn't wish Connor O'Connor on my worst enemy."

"Oh. So, is that what I am?" Mallory asked,

with a bit of a smile.

I shrugged. There was a smile tugging at my lips too, but I wasn't going to let it out.

A few minutes later, the bookshop staff started packing up, apologising to everyone who was still waiting. Connor O'Connor didn't apologise. He just went and sat in the front of the car outside.

"He could have stayed a bit longer," Mallory said, looking at her unsigned book.

"'Course he could," I said. "He might be a world-famous author, but he's also a world-class pain."

"So, where's the present?" Dad asked when I climbed into our car.

"I'll have to get something else," I said. "I've worked out why he lives on his own private island. It's because nobody else will put up with him, but the poor animals don't have any choice."

Ellie was waiting when we arrived home. "You are so-o-o lucky!" she wailed. "It's not fair how lucky you are. You got to see Connor O'Connor, and I didn't. That's a once-in-a-lifetime opportunity, and I only get one lifetime."

"Don't worry, you didn't miss anything," I told her. "He's actually quite horrible."

I left the second-hand books stuffed under the front seat. Maybe I'd get them out again later. Then again, maybe I wouldn't even bother. It was funny how your opinion of people could change, once you got to know them better.

Chapter Thirty-three

A FEW DAYS LATER, WE FOUND A STACK OF computer boxes piled up in the corner of the classroom. This was exciting, until we realised it wasn't a delivery of brand-new computers, because all the boxes were empty.

We thought maybe we were done with Walls, and starting a new topic. The boys suggested it might be "Cardboard Box Engineering", which sounded like a fancy name for what we used to do in the junior block. Karl said it was probably more junk for the Recycling Team. To their disappointment, however, they were wrong. Mr Cool said we were going to build a replica of the Berlin Wall. One third of the class would be in East Berlin, one third would be in West Berlin, and the rest would be border guards and checkpoint officials.

There was a huge uproar, because all the boys wanted to be border guards, and nobody wanted to live in East Berlin, except for a few kids who couldn't remember which side was which.

"I have to live in West Berlin because I get asthma," Georgia announced.

"I have to live in West Berlin so I can keep up my swimming training," Claudine said.

"I have to live in West Berlin because I get withdrawal symptoms if I can't go shopping." That was Jessica, surprise, surprise.

"Me, too!"

"And me!" That was Renee and Latisha.

Mr Cool said he would decide who was going to live where, and he wasn't open to bribes under a thousand dollars. He pulled some of the desks apart and made a line with masking tape down the middle of the room. Then he said we would all build the wall together before he split us up into groups, and he wouldn't tell us beforehand which side of the room was going to be East and which would be West.

"This side over here *is* east," said Callum, who was good at maps and knew things like that.

"We're not bound to exact geographical imperatives," Mr Cool said. Callum looked blank. He was good at maps, but not at long words.

"I'm not telling you beforehand," Mr Cool said, "because if you make the wall too easy to climb over, and then you end up in West Berlin, you're going to be swamped with refugees, and you won't like that. Or you might be a border guard, in which case you'll need the wall to be secure, or people will escape and you'll get into trouble."

"Which side are *you* going to be on, Mr Cameron?" Zoe asked.

"I've already been to Eastern Europe," Mr Cool said. "Years ago, with my girlfriend. So I'll stay in the West, I think."

"Was that Carmen?" Zoe said.

"No, actually," Mr Cool said.

"Can the guards have guns?" Matt said.

"No," Mr Cool said.

"Not even pretend ones?" Matt asked, shooting off a pretend one.

"No," Mr Cool said.

It took ages to build our Wall, because the boys took it so seriously. Lots of little kids came and stood in the doorway, open-mouthed, watching the construction process. When it was finally done, Mr Cool took us out into the playground and divided us into three groups.

I just knew I was going to end up in East Berlin. My life this year was clearly pointing in that direction.

"You people go and find a desk on that side of the room," Mr Cool said, indicating a group with Jessica in the middle of it. "You are going to be living in West Berlin."

"*Yes!* Shops! Cafes! Restaurants! Consumer goods!" shrieked Jessica.

"That's not fair," Aleesha said. "What about me? I want to be with Jessica."

"Sorry," Jessica said. Her group marched triumphantly back inside to take possession of West Berlin.

"You're going to be patrolling the wall and guarding Checkpoint Charlie." Mr Cool separated another group off. "And you lot are going to be in East Berlin," he said, pointing at the rest of us.

"Aw, no, come on!" Matt said. "I'm totally made to be a guard!"

There was more uproar when we got back inside. East Berlin was darker than West Berlin, because West Berlin had more windows. We hardly had any paper to write on, and we didn't have enough chairs.

"This isn't fair," Aleesha said. "I want to swap with someone."

"You can't do this," Callum protested. "East Berlin is on the west side of the room!"

"Mr Cameron," Karl bleated, "my desk's on the other side of the wall!"

"Right," Mr Cool said, "you've discovered that your workplace is on one side of the city and your home is on the other. What are you going to do?"

"Um ... not do any work?" Karl said.

"Well, that's one possibility," said Mr Cool, "but in that case you're going to run out of money pretty quickly and you'll probably get kicked out of your home as well."

"No, I won't," Karl said, lifting the lid of the nearest desk. "This house is owned by an evil money-grubbing landlord from West Berlin, and I bet she's not going to come over here to collect the rent."

"Ew, Karl, get your dirty hands off my desk," Latisha squealed.

"Only if you swap places," Karl said.

"Live in East Berlin? No thanks," Latisha said. "You can have it."

A few people tried to escape, but the border guards fired paper darts at them and rebuilt the bits of wall that collapsed. All the best stuff was in West Berlin: the computers, the telephone, the dvd player, the digital camera, the whiteboard, the library corner. Mr Cool laid out bowls of chips, dips, biscuits and plastic glasses of lemonade on his desk, and we had to look on helplessly while the West Berliners scoffed all the yummy stuff. All we got was dry crackers and water. I bet Tina would have given us something, but she was away that day. The others seemed to adjust to their new lifestyle very quickly. They didn't even bother to toss any biscuits over the wall in our direction.

All we had to keep us occupied were a few packs of cards. We tried to draw graffiti on our side of the wall, but the guards wouldn't let us get too close. We were hungry and bored. Callum played sad country music on his air guitar. Life in East Berlin was grim.

It was a grumpy lunch hour. Out in the playground, we weren't divided up any more, but the West Berliners and the guards had had a good morning, while the rest of us were sick and tired of the whole thing.

"Can we swap sides now?" one of the East

Berliners asked after lunch. But Mr Cool said we couldn't. He said that would be tampering with history, and the fact that we weren't enjoying it much proved that we were learning a lot.

I thought we had learned quite enough, like how mean and selfish the West Berliners were. If I'd been over in West Berlin, I would have helped some of the East Berliners to escape. At the very least, I would have organised some petitions and got a few TV crews in to expose their inadequate standard of living.

Jessica was so busy talking to Renee and Latisha, she hadn't even looked over the Wall. It seemed like a long time now since we'd been best friends. And looking back, it occurred to me that I'd initiated all the fun we'd ever had. If I suggested something, Jessica said *all right,* or *yeah let's,* or *that sounds fun.* She was fun to do stuff with, but she never thought of anything by herself.

Let's go down to the shops. Okay.

Let's have a milkshake. All right.

Let's rob a bank and spend the money on a sports car like Mr Cool's. Yeah, good idea.

It got a bit boring, having to think up all the good ideas all the time.

Chapter Thirty-four

I DECIDED TO SIT AT MY OWN DESK – AT LEAST I still had that – and draw for the rest of the afternoon. I kept working on my world map. There were seahorses, octopuses and brightly coloured tropical fish now, amongst the whales and dolphins. As far as I was concerned, presentation was every bit as important as content.

Then something tickled my ankle. "*Psst*!" someone said. It was Mallory, crouched under the row of desks, with her fingers up to her lips.

"Come down here, but make sure nobody sees you," she whispered.

I had a quick look round. The West Berliners were watching a dvd on modern-day Germany.

The screen was placed at the wrong angle for us, and we had to crane our heads to see it. The guards were busy restocking their supply of paper darts. I ducked down and crawled along behind Mallory, suddenly realising that I'd hardly seen her all day. I would have thought she was off sick, like Tina, if it weren't for a vague impression of her being there when Mr Cool divided us all up.

"What are you doing down here?" I whispered back. And then I saw. Mallory had made a little den in a corner of the wall, hidden behind desks and chairs and a rug, and she'd set up a secret cache of goods. She had Jessica's good felt pens, and coloured paper, a pile of library books, chips, scissors and Sellotape.

"Cool!" I said, deeply impressed, but trying not to show it. "Where did you get all this stuff from?"

Mallory grinned. "Have a guess."

"Um – you came inside at lunch time and took it?"

"The classroom was locked at lunch time. Look." She carefully wiggled a few boxes aside. "I built this bit of the wall. See, if you know how it's designed, you can tunnel through under Mr Cool's desk. The guards are so busy looking for people climbing over the top, they never even notice."

Now I was even more impressed. "How many times have you been through?"

Mallory shrugged. "Two or three."

"Wow! Can I—?" *Can I have a go too*? I was going to say. But then I stopped. What I heard myself say was, "Why are you telling me all this?"

Mallory grinned again. "I wouldn't wish East Berlin on my worst enemy," she said.

"So, is that what I am?" I asked. It was a serious question, or at least it started off that way, but I could feel myself starting to smile as well.

It was easy to tunnel through without being caught. Everyone was too busy watching the film to notice us, and the soundtrack covered any noise we made. We took turns. Mallory got the roll book. I took a pile of notices waiting to be given out and the digital camera. There was one sticky moment when Mr Cool stopped the dvd to ask questions about it, but I sat at the back with my head down, and nobody spotted me.

"I think we should mobilise now, don't you?" Mallory said.

But the East Berliners were dopey with boredom, and counting the minutes till the bell went for the end of school. It was hard to get them interested.

"You can't just take this situation sitting down!" I said. "Stand up for justice and your rights! The whole thing is deeply unfair. Those West Berliners have had a cushy time. Why should they get the best of everything? They're no different from us!"

"Shut up!" shouted someone from West Berlin. "We're trying to watch this!"

"See?" I said. "We need equal rights. Equal opportunities."

"Equal viewing rights for movies!" Callum agreed.

"We'll be shot," Claudine objected.

"You need to take risks for the sake of freedom," Mallory said. "First of all, we use our secret stash of equipment to make the outside world aware of our plight." She handed out the notices and felt pens. "Scribble a message for help, and we'll pass them out through the window. We'll drop a few over the Wall as well, in case there are people over there who want to help us."

"But these are notices about next week's cross-country trials," Karl objected.

"Write on the back of them!" I said. "Show some counterintelligence for once."

"Don't let the guards see what you're doing,"

Mallory instructed. "Get in small groups and pretend you're playing cards or noughts and crosses. Plus, we're going to take photos of the miserable conditions behind the Wall, and smuggle them out."

"How? We haven't got the digital camera," Aleesha said.

"Yes, we have," said Mallory, producing it.

It was twenty to three. The dvd was finished, and Mr Cool said the West Berliners could have free time until the bell went. Tomorrow, he said, we'd have a class discussion on how we felt about our wall experiment.

"Suckers!" someone yelled over the Wall at us.

"Yeah, glad we're not stuck in East Berlin," someone else sniggered.

"Just you wait," Matt said, "we're going to—" but I elbowed him to shut up.

We stationed Callum and Georgia at the window, handing out notices to anyone going past. Two other kids stood behind them, to shield them from the border patrol. Other kids were stationed at intervals along the Wall, getting ready to drop their messages over. Aleesha was talking to the guards at Checkpoint Charlie. They were bored by now, too, and more interested in Aleesha than in what was going on behind the wall.

Mr Cool was scrabbling round on his desk. “Has anyone seen a pile of—?”

“I think we better make our move soon,” I murmured to Mallory.

But we didn’t have to. At ten to three, the door opened and a whole crowd of people came pouring in: all the kids from Rooms Eight and Ten, and their teachers, and a few parents who’d turned up early, and Esther from the school office, and a teacher aide with her special needs kids. Lots of them were holding our notices. Right at the back, but making the most noise, was Mr Bennett. He was holding one of our notices in one hand. The other hand was holding a brochure advertising *21 days of sun soaked bliss on board the luxurious Sea Princess.*

“What’s all this?” he bellowed. “What’s going on here? Human rights abuses? Discrimination? Unfair treatment?”

“Yeah, and we didn’t get any chips, either,” Karl said.

“All I’ve got is a sheet of noughts and crosses,” said a puzzled parent.

Mallory leapt up onto my desk. “It’s all true!” she cried. “We in East Berlin call the world to witness the flagrant abuse of human rights being carried on right here in this classroom.

People are being discriminated against. Picked on. Even shot!"

Mr Bennett was busy assuring the parents that this was all an exaggeration, and that the school had a strict anti-bullying policy. Meanwhile, the East Berliners started throwing more messages over the wall. Some of the West Berliners darted forward to pick them up and read them.

"Hey, you can't do that!" protested the guards.

"Too late! We *are* doing it." I leapt up onto the desk beside Mallory. "Come on," I shouted, and I threw down one of the top boxes. "The Wall's coming down, right now!"

"They're right," someone said in West Berlin. "We ought to help."

"I've got to take a picture of this," Mr Cool said. "Where's the camera?"

It took much less time to pull the Wall down than to build it, which was probably a deeply symbolic statement that Mr Cool was hoping someone would make the next day. The kids from Rooms Eight and Ten helped and so did the parents.

When the bell went, the boxes were all stacked up in a corner of the room, just like at the beginning of the day.

"That class discussion tomorrow is going to be interesting," Mallory said.

"More than interesting," Aleesha said, glowering at Jessica.

"I wanted to give you some chips, honest," Jessica said, "but the guards said I couldn't."

"Yeah, right," Aleesha said, flouncing off.

"*How* did you get the digital camera onto that side of the Wall, Mallory?" Mr Cool asked, but Mallory just shrugged.

"Don't you think it's better to leave some mysteries unexplained?" she said.

Mean and Nasty, Mean and Nasty, I tried to remind myself, but it was no use. Words like *imaginative, funny, smart* kept crowding them out.

If you can have second thoughts, are you allowed to have third thoughts? I didn't want to admit it, even to myself, but I was starting to like Mallory.

Mum might want to go and visit her old boss in prison, once the drug police swooped on him, but perhaps it wouldn't be so bad, running into Mallory at visiting hours. Maybe we could even carpool sometimes.

Chapter Thirty-five

"GOOD NEWS!" MUM WAS SMILING. "Theo phoned. He's coming home!"

"Brilliant! When?" I said.

"Not long ago, something to do with time differences, I think," Mum said vaguely.

"No, I mean, when is he coming home?"

"Four o'clock on Saturday afternoon. Won't it be good to see him again? I've really missed him, haven't you, Harry? And so have the cats, although I think they've got used to us at last." She bent down to scratch Lucy on the back of her head, and Lucy sank to the ground in a blissful daze.

I sank into a bit of a daze as well. The cats …

it *was* brilliant that Uncle Theo was coming back, of course it was, and I had missed him too, but Uncle Theo coming back meant the cats going back – and I'd loved having them at our place.

"Hey, great news, everyone," Mallory said. "My dad's coming back this weekend."

"Lucky you," Aleesha said enviously. "He always brings you such cool stuff."

"I asked for a new a watch this time," Mallory said, "and lots of cheap dvds—"

"Counterfeit," I said coolly.

"What time's he arriving?" Jessica asked. "Can I come round and see what you got?"

"Four o'clock, Saturday," Mallory said. "I dunno. We might go out somewhere for a meal, I guess. We'll have lots to talk about."

For the first time, I wondered who looked after Mallory when her dad was away. I still didn't even know if her mum was around. But that thought was quickly overlaid by another. Four o'clock, Saturday? Uncle Theo and Mr Woz must be on the same flight!

Ellie asked to come with us to the airport. "Please?" she begged. "I never get to go anywhere, and otherwise I'm going to have the most boring day in my whole entire life."

The Arrivals hall was pretty full. Several flights were due in at the same time, and lots of people were standing around waiting. There were some sports-looking people in uniforms and some TV people with cameras. One woman walked past where we were standing and said loudly to her friend, "Oh, just look at that girl with the wonderful hair."

What girl? I turned round to look too, but there was no one there. When I turned back, the lady's friend was smiling right at me.

Was it *me* they meant? Me, with wonderful hair? Surely not.

"Look," Ellie whispered loudly, "there's M and N M."

"Who?" I said.

"Mean and Nasty Mallory," Ellie whispered, even more loudly. "And look, isn't that your Mr Cool from school?" She obviously liked the sound of that. "Mr Cool from school, Mr Cool from school," she chanted under her breath.

"What?" I said. Mallory had seen us but she had her arms folded and was definitely not waving. An older girl stood beside her, tall and long-legged in jeans and a purple jacket with an orange bandanna wound round her head,

and next to her was – Ellie was right – Mr Cool. *What's he doing here?*

I must have said it out loud, because Ellie said, "I'll go and ask."

"No!" I said. "You can't, you don't even know him," but a small thing like that wasn't going to deter Ellie. She darted off before I could stop her.

Half a minute later she was back. "That girl is Mallory's sister," she reported. "Her name's Carmen, and she's—"

"Mr Cool's girlfriend!" I gasped in astonishment.

Ellie nodded vigorously.

"No! That's not possible! She can't be! She's not Spanish!"

I was still trying to adjust to these new-and-unexpected relationship patterns when someone tapped me on the shoulder. Actually it was more like a whack than a tap, which was understandable, given that it was Karl who was doing the whacking (or tapping).

"What are you doing here?" he said, grinning.

"Ah – I dunno. Queuing up for an icecream? Buying the groceries? Or maybe – ooh, let's see – waiting to meet someone off a plane? What are *you* doing here?"

"Meeting my brother," Karl said. "He's been on this trip thing. Hey," he said, "I was gonna ask if you want to—"

"What?" I said, looking over his shoulder to where the first passengers were starting to come out, pushing trolleys piled high with luggage.

"Hey, Karl! Wotcha doing talking to a girl?" yelled a voice. It was another Ballentyne brother. I hadn't seen Karl's brothers for a while, and this one was about ten times as big as I remembered. He was tall and muscled, and surprisingly good-looking. Would Karl ever get to look like that?

Karl went bright red (which was very interesting to watch, like a speeded-up sunset). He went so red that I was wondering how hot his face would have to get before the gel in his hair started to melt, and whether that would make a good experiment for the Science Fair.

"C'mon, you moron, get over here," the Ballentyne bro yelled.

"Well, um, I'll check with you later," Karl mumbled, but I still wasn't sure what he was going on about.

"Hey, he likes you!" the Ballentyne bro called out, squashing Karl into a wrestle hug and dragging him away, and Karl went even redder, which I hadn't thought was possible.

"He's using sarcasm," Karl yelled over his shoulder, but his brother muffled him before he could add anything else.

"Is your uncle coming yet?" Ellie kept asking. "I never get to meet anyone at the airport. It's so exciting to be having an exciting day for once. Is that him?"

"Ellie, that person looks nothing like Uncle Theo," I said. "Use your eyes, not your mouth."

"I can't help it, I've never seen him before," Ellie said. "Is that him?"

"Yes!" I yelled. "There he is, that's Uncle Theo!" and I launched myself at him at a flying run. It was *so* good to see him again.

"Harry, my dear, good to see you," he said, giving me a hug. "Goodness me, I think you've grown. Em, Jack – and who's this? Ellie? Pleased to meet you. What a welcoming committee!"

For a while there was a confused babble of noise and excuse-me's, as everyone tried to talk at once, and other people tried to squeeze past. Then I saw Mallory racing towards her dad and his overladen luggage trolley.

Nobody else had noticed. The conversation was still a babble of "How was your flight?" and "Is this all the luggage you've got?" and "How are the cats?"

Uncle Theo was busy assuring Mum that he hadn't lost his luggage, passport or any weight. "I managed to find my way about very nicely, thank you," he said. "And how is school going?"

"School is extremely boring, thank you for asking," Ellie said.

"Oh look ... there's the Ballentynes, I haven't seen them for ages," Mum said, waving happily. "And there's Alex, over there, look!"

Mr Woz waved back and changed direction to head towards us, Mallory pushing the luggage trolley, and big sister Carmen walking along behind with Mr Cool. There were a lot of introductions, which Mallory and I both kept well out of.

Surely he wasn't going to get away with it. And he *was* getting away. Not a movie-style getaway, with racing cars and screaming tyres, but he was still getting away scot-free. His luggage was bound to be stuffed full of dangerous drugs (not to mention smuggled birds' eggs and counterfeit dvds) and nobody was doing anything about it.

Wait! The sniffer dogs were coming. Two little beagles, led by two airport officials. The beagles were sniffing excitedly, pulling on their leads. The officials were chatting to each other. They weren't even noticing the dogs' excitement. They were going to walk right past!

"Come on then, let's get going," Dad said.

"No, wait! Wait!" I said.

My wild imagination had taken off. It was tearing across the wide-open African landscape like a roaring lion, and I was the helpless antelope frozen in its path. No, that wasn't right. It was zooming off into space like a rocket and I was being pulled along behind in the slipstream. That wasn't it, either. It was rattling away at top-speed, like ... like .... The point was, my imagination was dragging me after it, and I was helpless to resist.

"Harry!" Mum said. "Come on, we're all waiting for you."

The drug-sniffer dogs stopped in their tracks. They lifted their drug-sniffing noses and pointed them straight at Mallory's dad. The TV crews raced towards him, waving microphones and pointing cameras as if on the way to the scoop of the century. Police appeared from all directions. They grabbed him, wrestled him to the ground, clipped handcuffs onto him and led him away to a waiting police car while everyone stood round and stared, open-mouthed. Mr Woz tried to yell something over his shoulder to Mallory, but the police pushed him into the van and drove off with tyres squealing.

You know what?

That didn't even happen.

You know what did happen?

The sniffer dogs caught a whiff of something, sure enough, and they followed it, dragging the airport officials behind them. They sat at my feet, happily wagging their tails and looking pleased with themselves, having tracked down *my* bag – *my bag* that was stuffed full of half-eaten chocolate bars and disgusting bits of left-over and forgotten-about lunch.

"Got some contraband in there, have you?" said one of the customs men, grinning.

Chapter Thirty-six

I DIDN'T WANT TO SEE ANYONE AFTER THAT ultra-embarrassing episode, but everyone came back to our place; Mum invited them all. Uncle Theo came. Mallory's entire family came, including Mr Cool, although he wasn't strictly family – or not yet anyway. Karl and his obnoxious brothers came, and his dad who was surprisingly nice, considering he had Karl as a son. I hadn't seen him for ages but I recognised him, of course. I've known him almost as long as I've known Karl; he used to come and do parent help at kindergarten when he was working shifts.

The Bucklers turned up, bringing homemade

bread and two sorts of soup because Mrs Buckler was so embarrassed at Ellie inviting herself to come with us. (Ellie, of course, wasn't embarrassed at all.) There was pumpkin, and tomato, which was lucky because I hate pumpkin. Adam followed them in, book in hand, sank into a chair and kept reading.

They all came, and they all laughed their heads off about the sniffer dogs sniffing out the rotten apples and week-old ham sandwiches that I'd forgotten to throw out of my bag.

"And you should have seen the look on Harry's face," Dad chuckled. "Absolutely flabbergasted. Did you think they were going to arrest you for drug smuggling or something, Harry?"

"No, not *me!*" I said, a bit too quickly, and a bit too loudly. Then I realised what I'd said, but it was too late. The words were out of my mouth. There was one of those sudden gaps that sometimes happen in conversation, and everyone was staring at me. Karl Ballentyne was grinning his head off. I wished his head *would* fall off and roll away.

"Then who?" said Dad, sounding like the rhyme about the cookie jar.

There were about sixteen people squashed into our tiny living room, and sixteen people not talking can make an awful lot of silence. Fifteen people all looking at the sixteenth person can make for an awful lot of sticky embarrassment.

"Nobody!" I said. And I tried my hardest to keep my eyes fixed on Dad, but I couldn't help it, I couldn't stop them from sliding over to Mr Woz. (Sliding eyes, another gross idea to add to creeping flesh and oozing brains.)

Everyone else looked too.

"What? *Alex* isn't a drug dealer!" Mum said, astonished.

"Harry! Where did you get *that* idea from?" said Dad.

"Harry ..." said Mr Cool, laughing. "I think you've really let your imagination run too far this time, haven't you?"

Everyone was staring at me, and my face had gone even redder than Karl's. Someone at the back of the room hooted with laughter. Mum looked cross. Dad looked amused, Mr Woz looked puzzled and Mallory looked – what *was* the expression on her face?

Only an hour or so ago, I had thought being targeted by cute little beagles was the most embarrassing thing that could happen to me. I was so wrong. *This* was, quite possibly, my most embarrassing episode *ever*, in a life that was littered with them. At the moment when I desperately needed a fast-forward button, my personal time frame had not just jammed, it was stuck on rewind.

No, not me!

Then who?

Nobody!

What? Alex isn't a drug dealer!

Harry! Where did you get that idea from?

In years to come, my high school yearbook entry would read: Person Most Likely to Embarrass Herself in Public. I would star in a reality TV show called *Foot in Mouth*, the camera perched on my shoulder, with the embarrassing situation hurtling towards me at full speed. Everyone watching at home would be able to see it coming, but I'd just march right in there.

My imagination had been rattling away at top-speed like a runaway train, because it was a runaway imagination. And that was exactly what *I* felt like doing: running out the door and never coming back.

It turned out that Mr Woz and Mr Page weren't drug dealers or bird smugglers at all. They might have been greasy and slimy and totally unpleasant, but they weren't actual criminals.

They did go overseas a lot, but that was only because they were highly paid lawyers, and they went to Thailand to visit Mr Page's brother who worked there. The brother was a doctor in a refugee camp (which just goes to show that the general unpleasantness can't have contaminated the whole family). They even sent money to help support the hospital at the refugee camp, which was why there were bank statements in the mail from a Thai bank.

What's more, beagles aren't even drug sniffer dogs. The real drug sniffer dogs are much bigger and meaner looking. Beagles sniff around for fruit and other food that people aren't supposed to bring into the country, and they don't work in the public areas, just in the Customs Halls, but my leftover lunch smells must have been too exciting to ignore. And the TV crews were there to meet a returning under-19 soccer team – including Karl's brother – which I might have known about if I'd ever paid attention to the weekend sporting results.

"He still *looks* evil," Ellie said in an undertone.

"Phrenology," Adam said. "A nineteenth century science, popular in Victorian times. Phrenologists thought you could tell what people were like by measuring and feeling the bumps on the outside of their skull. It was supposed to tell you whether they were criminals or geniuses or whatever."

"Did it work?" I asked.

"No," Adam said. "Later the theory was discredited."

Only Adam would say "discredited" instead of "wrong".

Whatever. In other words, Mr Woz might look like a criminal, but that didn't necessarily make him one. He wasn't trying to keep an eye on us when he dropped Mum home from work. He was just dropping Mum off on *his* way home, because he liked to have dinner with Carmen and Mallory before going back to the office for a few hours.

"I still can't believe that Carmen is Mallory's sister," I said.

"Six degrees of separation," said Adam. Ellie and I looked at him. "The theory that you can always find a connection between any two people in the world, by no more than six other people. Like, someone might have gone to school with your aunty's neighbour's cousin. So what seem like coincidences aren't particularly unusual."

But in Carmen's case, this was only about

two degrees: totally, unbelievably weird. And Mallory had never let on.

Mr Woz wasn't spying when he came round. He was just seeing if our place was good enough for his precious (and paranoid) Blue Streak. He might have been snoopy and sly, as well as being greasy and slimy and smarmy and totally unpleasant, but he wasn't a spy. He was just nosey.

And they offered Mum a job because they hadn't wanted to advertise and get swamped with applications, so they asked the law school if they could recommend anyone, and the law school recommended Mum. Mr Page and Mr Woz were old friends from when they went to law school together. They started up their own law firm when Mr Woz, Carmen and Mallory moved from another town. That was when he and Mallory's mum split up and she went overseas, which was also when he took up smoking again, although he was trying to quit.

So, basically, I had totally messed up, and whenever I saw Mr Woz from now on, I was going to feel not insect-sized, but microscopic. I was very glad when they left, soon after my foot-in-mouth episode. Mallory didn't look at me so I had no idea what she was thinking. Mr Cool looked as though he thought the whole thing was hilarious.

The Ballentynes left at the same time. Mr Ballentyne said he was already running late for work, but it had been good to catch up with everyone, and we must do it more often. (*No way*, I thought.)

"See you soon, Harry," I thought he called, but it was hard to hear because Karl was concentrating so hard on trying to keep an equal distance from me and his two grinning brothers that he wasn't watching where he was going, and he tripped over Max in the hallway. Then his brother tripped over Karl, and his other brother did as well. His brothers had such enormous feet that poor Max nearly got flattened. He screeched and yowled and dodged his way back up the hallway, where Karl's dad tripped over him too.

"Karl Hubert Ballentyne!" his dad roared over all the screeching and yowling. "For gawd's sake, watch where you're going!"

Hubert? Karl's middle name was *Hubert*? How had he kept that secret from me?

"He's joking, it's a joke," Karl tried desperately to convince me.

"No way, man," said his soccer-team brother. "Ancient family name. Handed down, you know, like traditional. You're so lucky, I wish I was called—"

"Shut up!" Karl yelled.

Once they'd gone, the noise level dropped considerably. Uncle Theo looked at Dad and Mr Buckler, beaming. "Well! Good to hear that you two are going into business together," he said.

"You're *what*?" I said.

Dad nodded and grinned. "Always wanted to be a sparky," he said. "I'm going to be his apprentice."

"At *your* age?" I said.

"Why not?" Dad said. "Your mum retrained, at her age. I'm still a spring chicken. And no more of your cheek, or I'll zap you."

Ellie giggled. "You could call yourselves the Bright Sparkies."

My dad the electrician. It was certainly turning out to be a day of surprises.

"What happened to *you can't teach an old dog new tricks*?"

"Woof, woof!" Dad said.

"Anyway, we're thinking of expanding the business," Mr Buckler said. "Given your dad's expertise with building and car maintenance, we might market ourselves as *Two* Jacks of All Trades."

"And I can help support your mother," Dad went on.

"Mum already has a job," I said. "She doesn't need support."

"I do have a job," Mum said. "But I'm not sure if it's the right one for me. I'd like to be involved in something where it feels like I'm helping people more. Unless, that is, I can persuade the firm to take in a bit more legal aid work."

Persuade Mr Woz to do things to help other people? Doubt it. But who knows? Dad had found a job at last. Who knew what else might happen?

The surprises still weren't over.

"The cats seem to have enjoyed their visit," Uncle Theo mused. "Tilda looks as though she'd be happy to stay, and I'm sure your house is more entertaining for a kitten than mine. But there's still a catch, isn't there? The thing about your father and animals."

"Oh, well," Dad said nonchalantly, "we might be able to find a way around that." And he bent down and *patted* a cat that was strolling past.

And not just *any* cat. It was Cleo – and she just let him do it.

"Well, while everyone else is dishing out surprises, I've got one too," said Adam.

"Your film!" Ellie shrieked. "You won! I said you were going to win!"

"No, I didn't win," Adam said, "but I came third ... and the top three all go forward to the national School Film Championships. The judge said I showed definite potential, and that he couldn't promise anything, but I could apply for a job with his studio in ten years' time, if I'm still into film then."

"Who judged it?" said Ellie. "Was it someone famous? Was it Peter Jackson?"

Adam pretended to zip up his mouth. "Can't say."

"We'd better have a look, then," Dad said. Mr Buckler did something clever with rigging up a projector to the computer. We all found seats, on the sofa or the chairs or on the floor. Adam's movie rolled up onto the screen.

"It's only a few minutes long," he said apologetically. "Don't expect an epic."

"It *is* epic," Dad said. "Adam Buckler's first film. We're watching history here."

I would have been happy to watch the longest film ever made, because I was so relieved to have the attention taken off me for a while, but I wondered which cat was going to have its future blighted by being cast as the villain. But it wasn't about serial killers at all.

"It was those shots from Forest Road," Adam whispered. "I started to think about snooping, and spying . . ."

The film's title appeared: *The cat who came in from the cold.*

"From the cold?" Ellie said, puzzled. "Is it a documentary or a weather forecast?"

"Spy story," Adam said.

He must have spent hours filming, trying to catch the right shots. He captured the cats in all the right situations, and then edited the scenes very cleverly. Max nosed up to Alfie, and Alfie rubbed heads with Lucy, and Lucy padded past Cleo, one after the other, as though passing on a message. Tilda peered round a corner and skittered away, as though she was on guard and warning the others of someone's arrival.

Mum was the baddie scientist, and the cats were trying to get hold of a new brand of cat food, which she was secretly developing in her kitchen laboratory. It all ended happily with a shot of Oscar blissfully snoozing in the sun, next to an empty cat food tin. The credits rolled, and everyone clapped.

"Very good, Adam," Uncle Theo said.

"Look, it says thanks to me," Ellie cried.

"There's my name up on screen!"

"Thanks to my sister Ellie," I read out, "for occasionally stopping talking long enough to let me think."

"What about Harry? You should have thanked her for something," Ellie said.

"I did," Adam said.

"Unlimited thanks to Harriet Jasmine Emerald Florence Mabey McDonald," Dad read out, "famous for her unlimited imagination."

Chapter Thirty-seven

THE BIGGEST SURPRISE WAS FINDING THAT Mallory didn't hate, scorn or despise me. She seemed to find it quite funny that I'd suspected her father of being involved in the drug or bird smuggling trade. And she took it for granted that we were going to be friends from now on. A few days later, she turned up after school: just walked up the path, knocked on the door and breezed in as soon as I opened it.

"What are you doing here?" I asked. "Aren't you supposed to be out shopping or something?"

"Nah. Boring. Come to help with the cats instead," she said.

Not *Can I help?* or *Do you mind if I help?* For a moment I felt myself bristling like a hedgehog. "Sure, you can clear out all the litter trays," I said.

"Generous offer," Mallory said. "Actually, I was thinking more of stretching out in a hammock with a cat on my lap, while you brought me cold drinks and chocolates."

"Sorry," I said. "No hammocks. And no chocolates."

"Sad," Mallory said. "But I guess I'll cope. You know," she added as we went out into the garden to look for the cats, "we could have been friends a long time ago if you hadn't been so mean to me."

"You mean, if *you* hadn't been so mean to *me*." She shook her head. "Aviaries?" I demanded, bristling up again. "Have you forgotten?"

Mallory punched me on the arm and grinned. "Can't you take a joke? Anyway, I got kidnapped by Jessica—"

"I didn't notice you trying to escape."

"—and you never paid any attention to me, because you were so obsessed with Karl Ballentyne."

"Excuse me?"

"So obsessed with—"

"I *heard* what you said." This time I punched her on the arm. Hard.

"You can see right into their house," Mallory realised a moment later. Ellie was shrieking in the next-door garden with a group of friends. She gave us a quick wave and then went back to the game they were playing.

"Where's ah ...?"

"A–A–Adam? He's gone off to do some research at the library – into the history of filmmaking. They might come round later. Or tomorrow."

"That's okay, I'll come back tomorrow, too," Mallory said.

"To see me ... or Adam?" Mallory just grinned. "So is this official? Are we going to be, like, friends now?"

Mallory nodded. "I guess."

"I don't know. Because every time I see your dad, I feel two centimetres tall, or even less. And I'm not that tall as it is. I need every centimetre I can get."

"Don't worry, you won't have to see him much. He's usually at work. Or if he's at home he might be outside"– she looked sideways at me – " in the birdcage."

We both started to giggle. "What was the correct name for that again?" I asked.

"There's just one thing," Mallory said. "If we're going to be friends, you have to learn how to pronounce my surname properly."

"I would have learnt ages ago, if you'd had a normal surname like everyone else."

"Oh, right. A normal, boring surname like McDonald?" She didn't say anything more; just stood there with her arms folded, waiting.

"All right, then," I sighed. "Woz-Ziz-Click-Jetski?"

"No."

"Woz-Tik-Clikski? Woz … Woz … go on, just tell me!"

Mallory spelt it out, very slowly and clearly (and who'd have thought it would have a J in it?), then she repeated it for me, syllable by syllable. After ten minutes and nearly 500 repetitions, I nearly had it right.

"Why do you have to have such a ridiculous surname anyway?" I grumbled.

Mallory grinned. "I guess I was just born with it."

"So were you born with any other names? In between the Mallory and – that?" I didn't feel like tackling her surname again straightaway.

"You mean, like a middle name? Hundreds," Mallory said.

"You're joking."

"Well, what do you think? One, of course. Like every other *normal* person."

Phew. This time my sigh was one of relief. We could still have been friends if she'd had four middle names, but I was glad that she didn't.

On Monday morning, Mr Cool came into class wearing a sporty shirt and his baseball cap, long baggy shorts and green shoes.

"What do you think, Zoe?" he asked.

Zoe was staring, bug-eyed. She gulped and managed to find her voice.

"*Green* shoes? I didn't know they even made green shoes."

Mr Cool looked down at them critically. "Well, sneakers really. I don't think I'd go for green shoes myself. But sneakers are different, don't you think?"

"Did you choose them?" Zoe asked, hoping some new or existing girlfriend might be responsible, but Mr Cool said he did.

"They're all right," Karl said. "They're not green like puke, they're more lime green."

"Lime green *is* puke green," Callum said.

There was a short but intense debate about the relationship between lime green and puke green and how much it depended on what you'd been eating. We decided to forego news in favour of a class-wide vote about the shoes. It came in as almost equal for and against, with one not sure. That was Zoe, who spent the rest of the morning shaking her head and murmuring to herself, "Green shoes!" I wondered if this was the beginning of the end of MCAS.

I was heavily in favour, myself. It takes serious imagination to pick out and wear bright green shoes.

And that was exactly when it came to me – looking at Mr Cool's green shoes, and then at my Family Tree, still up on the wall with its green and red decorations, and thinking about Christmas – an idea! An idea for the Recycling – sorry, Futures – Team. My powers of imagination were still there! I hadn't lost them after all . . . or, worse, used them all up at the airport.

We'd hand out sheets of paper for an art competition – no, even better, we'd get one of the classes to make paper (recycling!) and we'd ask everyone to bring in all their old birthday and Christmas cards (more recycling!). Then we'd choose some of the best artwork, mount the pictures on (recycled!) card, and sell them as new cards.

“Pictures of rubbish bins?” said Karl, who didn’t quite get it.

“No! Well . . . maybe. Why not?”

Chapter Thirty-eight

LATER THAT DAY, MR COOL SAID HE WANTED a quiet word with me. *Uh-oh.* Was it going to be a word like *stupid* or *irresponsible* or *ridiculous*?

But it wasn't that at all.

"Harry, have you ever thought that you might have quite a gift for words?"

"Ah … no," I said. "I do Art, remember? And after that I do Animals. Not English."

"Well, I'm not so sure," said Mr Cool. "What about that writing competition I was telling you about a few weeks ago? I think I've got some spare copies of the entry form," he said, fossicking around among the teetering piles on his desk. "Somewhere in here … where are they

. . . how is it that things just vanish, sometimes? Do you ever find that, Harry?"

"All the time," I said, although now I came to think about it, I hadn't lost so many things just lately.

"Ah – here we are." He pulled out a sheet of A4 and handed it over. "You've got a good imagination; you should be able to come up with something. Just have a go."

I still hadn't quite got over the fact that Mr Cool's girlfriend was Mallory's sister. Talk about truth being stranger than fiction; I would never have imagined that. Did that mean I'd finally reached the limits of my imagination, the way that people in olden times used to think they would reach the edge of the world and fall off if they kept on sailing?

"Mr Cool might end up as your brother-in-law one day. Weird," I said to Mallory.

"Scary," she said. "And by the way," she added, "Claudine's got a swimming meet on this week."

"So?"

"So I think it's about time you played a game for us."

"What do you mean, a game?" I said suspiciously.

"I mean a game for the Hawaiian Hula Hulas."

"Ha! If that's what you think, then you haven't been at this school long enough. Don't you know by now that I don't do sport?"

"That's what *you* think," Mallory said. "But all that is about to change."

"I don't do sport," I said, "and I *especially* don't do netball. I'm too short."

Mallory looked at me as though she was measuring me up. "Do you know, I think you've got a bit taller lately."

"Really?"

"Nah," Mallory said, "just kidding. But don't worry about it. You can wear high heels more often if you're shorter, *and* you get more choice in boys."

So, here we are, a week later, on the indoor netball court. Actually *on* the court, rather than looking on from the sidelines, which is what Tina is doing. I always thought this would be hugely embarrassing, because it would be obvious that I had no skills at all and no idea of what I was meant to be doing, but I've survived so much embarrassment lately that this feels like nothing in comparison.

Adam turns up unexpectedly just as we're about to start. Unexpected by me, anyway, but Mallory doesn't look surprised. He's carrying a book, but it's not about mathematics, or astronomy, or ancient Egypt, or even why the dinosaurs became extinct. It almost looks like a *real* book; like a novel. Where did he get *that* from? I didn't think Adam knew that fiction existed.

"Is it good?" I reach over to have a look just before the game starts, and Mallory starts yelling at me to hurry up. There's a name written in large, swooping handwriting on the inside page – Mallory's name.

Interesting.

You have to climb through a sort of door in the nets to get onto the court and I get all tangled up in it, which doesn't seem like a good start. Karl is laughing his head off at me, although Adam is deep in his book and not watching, not that I really mind what Adam thinks. (Does that mean I do mind what Karl thinks?)

I'm wearing a bib with A on it, which means I'm on Attack first quarter. This sounds seriously scary, but Mallory says that if I mess up, they can rescue the situation in the next three quarters. This is supposed to be reassuring.

I think I'd like to have an L for Learner on the back of my bib, like you can put on the back window of your car when you're learning to drive, but apparently they don't make those.

For the next quarter I'll be playing Centre, then Defence in the third before being subbed off for the last quarter. I ask if I can't be subbed off for the entire game, which sounds a whole lot more enjoyable, but Mallory says that wouldn't count as being part of the team. I say it would count enough for me, but she's not budging.

We are still discussing or maybe arguing about this when the referee's whistle goes for the start. This is possibly the first time in my life that I've heard a referee's whistle go from the point of view of a participant, not a spectator.

What on earth am I doing here?

The few times I've sat and watched with Tina, it's been obvious where each team was going wrong. We could see when they were all bunching together, or where they could have run into gaps, and it was easy to criticise when someone missed a goal, or took too many steps, or held onto the ball for too long. But now I realise that the game looks quite different from this perspective.

While I'm still thinking all this, and trying to take in such a significant lifestyle change, the game seems to have got away from me already. Mallory and Jessica, the two Centres, are zooming all over the place. Karl, the other Attack, is halfway down the court.

"Harry!" he yells, and suddenly the ball is hurtling in my direction. Somehow I manage to catch it, to my astonishment (and everyone else's) but I can't see anyone to throw it to. The people on the other team are all in the way. That can't be fair.

Help! What do I do with it? I think we need a system like in chess, where you could have secret signals about where you're going to throw the ball, but there isn't time to make any kind of signal.

"Here, Harry!" Karl yells again. He's got free, but when I throw the ball to him, the other Centre zooms in from nowhere and catches it. How did that happen?

All the action changes direction, which makes me feel a bit dizzy. The other team takes the ball back down to our goal, but this time Callum gets hold of it and sends it back.

Karl is already right down the end, standing in the goal circle, under the netball hoop.

"Go in the circle! You can go in the circle!" people are yelling. I look round to see who they're yelling at, and apparently it's me, so I go and stand near the hoop as well. Karl is lining up a shot, while these two giraffe-types – only with long legs instead of necks – try to block him. Then suddenly he does this unexpected bounce pass to me. It's unexpected by the two giraffes, but also by me, so I fumble and nearly drop it.

Okay, I've got the ball. Now what am I supposed to do?

"Shoot! Shoot!" people are yelling.

"Shoot, Harry!" Tina calls. "Come on, I know you can do it!"

She knows more than I do. Me, shoot a goal?

"Hurry up!" Karl yells. "You've only got three seconds!"

Only three seconds? Maybe the ref is being nice to me. Maybe she can tell it's my first ever game, even without an L on my bib, because I'm sure she's giving me more than three seconds, or maybe it just seems like a lifetime.

I line the ball up carefully, try to remember everything Mallory told me – and shoot.

It doesn't go in.

Of course not. That would be too much of a miracle.

But Karl gets it on the rebound ('rebound', see? – all this sporty vocabulary I didn't even know I had) – and tosses it back to me.

"Get it in this time, you moron," he yells.

I glare at him, and hurl the ball up at the hoop, not even bothering to aim properly.

This time it goes in.

You know what? That *does* happen! I don't know how, but it does.

Karl whoops and hollers and high-fives me. And when he does, something really weird happens, like when you touch a car door sometimes and get an electric shock. This kind-of-like-an-electric-shock feeling goes shooting all the way down my arm. Can you get an electric shock from touching the floor of an indoor netball court? I don't think so, because nobody else seems to have noticed anything.

It can't have anything to do with touching Karl ... can it?

Chapter Thirty-nine

BEING CENTRE IS JUST AS ALARMING AS being Attack. I hardly touch the ball, which is lucky as my hand is still stinging from Karl high-fiving it, and my arm is still recovering from the weird electric shock, and my head is still trying to work out why it felt so different from when Karl hit me in kindergarten. But I run around a lot and get absolutely shattered.

Time seems to move at a different rate on the court, because the six-minute quarters go quite quickly when I sit watching with Tina, but they take forever now I'm playing. Perhaps we are temporarily existing in another time zone. This is an intriguing theory that Adam would probably be interested in, and I might tell him about it later.

Being on Defence is okay, because our team is rescuing the situation, as Mallory predicted, and I don't have a lot to do. And being subbed off in the final quarter is fine because I have nothing at all to do, except get my breath back and cheer our team on with Tina, although oddly enough, I catch myself feeling I'd almost like to be out there on the court again with Karl.

With the team, I mean. Not Karl in particular. Of course not.

And of course that isn't going to happen, because they'll never ask me to play for them again. Not that I'd care about that ... would I?

It's very close. The other team is still ahead, 12–10. Then Matt shoots a goal. 12–11.

Tina is bouncing up and down on the seat beside me, too excited to sit still. Adam glances up, looks at the scoreboard, and actually stops reading. He even puts his book down.

One minute to go. A few parents have turned up, and are cheering us on. Karl's dad sits down beside me.

"Hello Harry," he says. "How are we doing?"

"12-11 to them," I say, sounding knowledgeable. "But we just got a goal."

"Hear you're coming down to the restaurant soon," Karl's dad says.

"Uh – what?"

"What is it – work interview or work experience or something?" Karl's dad is busy watching the action, so he doesn't notice my mouth drop open. "We'll make sure we give you all a good lunch, anyway."

"Oh – thanks," I mumble, wondering when Karl was going to get round to mentioning that. Has he asked the whole class along, or what? *Give you all a good lunch ...* who's the 'all'?

Back down to this end, they miss a goal. 43 seconds to go. Up the court again. 30 seconds. 27 seconds.

"Come on! Come on!" Tina chants.

Can we get another goal in 27 seconds? We need two goals to win, but a draw would be almost as good. They haven't lost a game all season, and I don't want to feel I made them lose this one, even if none of them says so. But two goals in 27 seconds?

One of their team trips over and the ref stops play to check she's all right, but the clock keeps going. 16 seconds. 12 seconds. We're not even inside our goal circle yet.

Then Aleesha shoots a two-pointer. A two-pointer is a goal you shoot from outside the goal circle, but it sounds a bit like a white pointer to me. I can almost see it, cruising through the air with a mean expression and its fin pointing up, and grazing the net with its rows of sharp teeth.

13–12 to us!

Tina jumps up and claps. Claudine cartwheels from one side of the court to the other, and somewhere a faint voice that sounds like Piper is calling "Yay! We won!"

Everyone looks hot and red-faced and sweaty. They tear off their bibs and climb out through the door in the netting. Karl takes a great swig out of his drink bottle and looks round for somewhere to sit down.

Not that I really care where he sits.

He grins at his dad, and sits down beside him, which happens to mean that he's beside me as well. "Great goal," he says to me.

"I told you she'd be a good player," Tina says, as pleased as if she'd shot it herself.

"It was just a temporary aberration," I say, looking sideways at Adam. Sometimes it's a distinct advantage to know someone who reads the dictionary.

Jessica gathers up her wardrobe of spare clothes and stuffs them all into her bag. "Gotta go," she says. "Meeting Renee and Tish. See ya, everyone. See ya, Harry."

That's a special, separate 'see ya', just for me.

"See ya," I say back, a bit surprised.

Jessica grins as she goes past. "Why didn't you listen to me, all those years? I always said there was no reason you couldn't play."

"Apart from her total lack of coordination, fitness and knowledge of the rules, you mean," Karl says, but I'm not listening to him. I'm listening to *all those years*. Things have changed between Jessica and me; we'll never be friends the way we used to be, but there's still something special there.

"Don't spend too much money," I call as an afterthought.

"Impossible!" Jessica yells back.

Mallory plumps down between Adam and me. "So are you on for next week?" she says.

"Of course she is," Tina says.

I roll my eyes. "What about *you*, Tina?"

"Me? I can't play netball," Tina says, giggling. "I never play it before in my life."

"Neither had I. Come on, Tina. If I can play, so can you."

The whole team is there by now, and they're all standing round Tina.

"Tina Tiger! Tina Tiger! Come on, Tina!" they chant.

Tina laughs and blushes and hides her face. "All right. I do it," she says, peeping through her hands.

Chapter Forty

"NOW, I THINK YOU'LL ALL ENJOY OUR next topic," Mr Cool said this morning. He looked enthusiastic, but nobody else did. Glum would be a better description, or apprehensive, or just plain bored. Callum strummed a few chords on his air guitar, without much energy, as though the air was particularly heavy today.

"I think you'll all enjoy it because, this time, I've decided to let you choose your own topics."

"What? Choose our own what?" Claudine asked, rushing in late as usual.

"You'll need to get it okayed by me first. And of course," he added, "you'll have to use your imagination."

"What?" Matt said, dismayed. "But what if you don't have any imagination?"

"Cardboard Box engineering! Yes!" Karl yelled.

I had a million ideas, straightaway. But while I was trying to sort them out in my head, I couldn't help noticing that half the class was zeroing in – on me.

"Hey, Harry, have you got a partner?"

"Harry, will you pair up with me?"

"Me, me, Harry! Please, pick me!"

So here we are again, another week later. On the court with the Hawaiian Hula Hulas, waiting for the game to start. Me *and* Tina.

And Karl. But that's totally irrelevant, of course; as is the fact that I'm going to his dad's restaurant for lunch on Saturday, with Mallory, Tina, Callum and Matt, or the fact that Karl and I have just been appointed newsreaders for our trip to the TV studio next week.

Once again I wonder, *What on earth am I doing here*? Me, Harriet Jasmine Emerald Florence Mabey McDonald. I don't *do* sport. Then I start thinking: when did this year start going wrong – and when did it start going right again?

Well, it all started with Mallory, of course.

Or maybe not. It might have started years ago, when Mum decided to go back and study, because if she hadn't graduated in law, she'd never have got a job in Mallory's dad's law firm, and I wouldn't have got the chance to exercise my imagination (which makes it sound as though my imagination is much more sporty than I am) by suspecting him of being an evil, drug-dealing, egg-smuggling lawyer.

Or maybe it started even further back than that. Maybe it started with Uncle Theo, and his love of cats. If he wasn't such a cat fanatic, we wouldn't have had to look after them when he went away for six months, and I might never have found out that Mallory had an unsuspected cat-loving side to her personality.

Of course, if Uncle Theo hadn't gone away, my imagination would never have run away with me . . . or not quite so far, anyway. Uncle Theo is always a good person to talk to. Everything seems so peaceful and calm around him that you can't help telling him things, and somehow he helps you to make sense of the messy, complicated parts of your own life, and even laugh at them sometimes. So maybe philosophy does have some practical uses, after all.

But now Uncle Theo has found his way home

again. In fact, a lot of things have been found lately. Mum and Dad have both found jobs, Tilda has found a home at our place. Adam has found a potential career in movie-making, Ellie has found some friends her own age, Jessica has found a couple of friends (Renee and Latisha) who are as clothes-obsessed as she is. I've found at least one person in the world who likes my hair, plus a way to get back at Karl Ballentyne, next time he teases me about my middle names. I think I could even unfreeze my time frame now and set it going on normal speed.

Tina is tugging on my arm. She giggles and twists her bib around so she can read the letter A. "I don't know how to play, Harry."

"Me, neither. Don't worry," I reassure her. "Just have a go."

And then the referee's whistle goes for the start.

again, to find a lot. I think it's [illegible]. Actually
lately Mum and Dad have both found [illegible]. The
Huff has found a home [illegible] great place. Mum has
found a potential career in [illegible] speaking. She
has found [illegible] towards her own [illegible]. Jessica has
found a couple of friends there, and [illegible]
who are [illegible] dressed as [illegible]. I've found
at least one person in the world who likes my
hair plus a way to get back at [illegible]
next time [illegible] middle [illegible].
I think I could [illegible] my [illegible]
and [illegible] going on normal [illegible].

Tina is tugging on my arm. She giggles and
twists her [illegible] around so she can read the letter
A. [illegible]

"Me, neither. Don't worry," I [illegible].
"Just love one."

And then the [illegible] whistle goes for the
start.